THE LAST MAP

JOHN NEWSOM

JFNBooks

LAST

This book is a work of fiction. Names, characters, places, and incidents are the product of the author's imagination or are used fictitiously. Any resemblance to actual events, locales, or persons, living or dead is coincidental.

Also by John Newsom

The Xtrodinaries Book 1 Theo Lord of the Fries

The Xtrodinaries Book 2 Rina Much Ado About Netting

Join the reading group at: JohnNewsom.com

To J.K.
May we always have time for one more adventure.

Part I

Chapter 1

Michael Jefferson is an interesting human being. Michael Jefferson thinks he can fly. I don't mean jump really, really far or hover in the air for a little while, Michael Jefferson thinks he can take one step, take off and fly. And he is completely serious.

He tries endlessly, in the bottom of his heart always expecting to boost up and explode into the sky. It never quite happens.

Actually, everyone who knows Michael Jefferson expects him to one day jump out of a second story window, fully expecting to fly and fall terribly to the ground, never to be heard from again.

This surely would happen if Michael's mother didn't constantly tell him whenever she sees him jumping off of anything higher than a kitchen chair trying to take flight, "If I ever see you jumping out of a second story window, I'll wring your neck."

Michael Jefferson, in his heart, knows he can fly, but he also knows that he can not make his neck ring and under no circumstances does he want to find out how his mother can. So Michael Jefferson makes do launching himself off of steps, and sofas, and coffee tables, and countertops, and toilet seats, and whatever else a typical flying human being might use to jump up into the sky.

Michael's mother, who doesn't really approve of his flight plans, even offered to buy Michael a trampoline on his last birthday and put it in the backyard to the left of the driveway so Michael could leap into the sky all day and night. Michael says, "Mom, trampolines just make you bounce very, very high. I can fly."

Now, Michael has never flown, and his old-old-old-old- old-old-old Uncle Tony always says to Michael, "If you keep jumping around off this stuff you're going to break your legs, the both of them." Then old-old-old-old-old-old-old-old Uncle Tony would mumble under his breath, "Crazy kids these days, think they can fly! Crazy kids!" Now old-old-old-old-old-old- old-old Uncle Tony is actually only twenty-nine years old, but they call him Ole' Eighty because he shuffles around slowly, waves his arms quickly, and points his fingers disgustedly when he talks, like an old-old-old-old-old-old-old-old man.

His nickname is actually Old[8] Tony. That's Old to The Eighth Power Tony. It was at one time pronounced more like Ole' Eight-Tee. Now the name has come to sound more like an interstate when it is pronounced by the family, O-80.

The family remembers the running joke in the Jefferson household when old-old-old-Grandma Cherry (who really was old, she was Michael's great grandmother) made a funny play on words when someone new to the family would be introduced to Uncle Tony by his nickname, "O-80," she would never miss a beat when she quickly followed up with, "and I-90."

This joke became a little less humorous when not more than one year ago old-old-old Grandma Cherry was just missed by a car that hydroplaned off a patch of water on the Interstate and spun into the Jefferson's back yard activating Grandma Cherry's heart condition right before it landed rather neatly in their unfilled swimming pool. Old-old-old grandma Cherry was never heard from again. Nevertheless, the name O-80 stuck, and old-old-old-old-old-old-old-old Uncle Tony never fails to show his seemingly old age as he shuffles around the Jefferson household on his way to the back guest house, which is actually a garage, where he lived. 0-80 also tells Michael, "If I ever see you jumping off of anything higher than a sidewalk curb, I'm going to wring your little neck, just as soon as I muster up the strength to catch you!"

That's what is good about family—a lot of strangeness can seem perfectly normal in the time and space of your own home. Michael takes all of the warnings he receives in stride. He continues to launch himself off low-lying household items, like his latest attempt off the arm of the living room couch, or the attempt before that off the leg of a kitchen stool. Michael always keeps an eye towards an open window or nearby door so when he does take flight he can head up into the sky. But so far Michael always comes back down to Earth, usually rather softly and gracefully, but nevertheless, he always comes back down to Earth, still knowing in his heart he can fly.

Chapter 2

M ichael, for the most part, gets away with his all day attempts at flying around the house because he is a good student. Michael is a very good student even though he spends his school days in the back of the classroom next to the windows in case he ever feels the need to take flight.

Michael does like school, and he usually stays focused on his daily lessons and not totally focused on flying while in school. He is especially focused on Fridays, the last period of the day, in Mrs. Grand's class. Friday's last period is always the time for the class game called Class-Wide Challenge. This weekly game places students on two teams. Each team sends a teammate to the front of the class to compete in one-on-one weekly knowledge questions to score a point for their team.

Each knowledge question is based on information from the week's lesson. The most exciting part is that each week the winning team wins the bag o' candy. When speaking of the bag o' candy, Mrs. Grand always says, "It's like a huge piñata, but because you are all so ravenous, we don't even need the stick around here. You just tear into the bag every week like a pack of wolves, and then I hope the sugar high wears off by Monday."

To be a bit more specific, once the weekly bag o' candy is won, the team captain from the winning team actually tears into the medium size garbage bag full of candy with some control. Then winning team members reach two hands into the open bag and grab as much candy as they can carry on the way out the classroom door to start their weekend. The team names are always the team captain's favorite color followed by the word leaders, "because everyone is a leader in this classroom," Mrs. Grand always says.

This week's lesson in Mrs. Grand's class had focused on nouns and verbs, geography, and plants. The weekly Class-Wide Challenge game between the gold leaders, Michael's team, and the red leaders is close. During the first round students answer questions about common nouns. Then there is a round about abstract nouns. Then concrete nouns. Now students are going back and forth naming proper nouns. Nouns are the general topic, but Mrs. Grand always makes the students really think about what they learn during the week.

Mrs. Grand states a general and a specific subject for each round of the game, like capital cities around the world, and students have to think fast. Students have a moment to answer and come up with a proper noun that fits the general subject and the specific type like Paris, Cairo, or Tokyo as a capital city of the world. In order to get a point, a correct answer matches both the general subject and specific type that is introduced by Mrs. Grand for that round. For the current round the general subject is naming a proper noun and the specific type of proper nouns being named are international rivers of the world.

The game is ending and the score is very tight. The latest point up for grabs is between Michael's gold team (represented by Neeka). Neeka is facing Roxanne who represents the red leaders. Both girls are in the center of the class circle and both girls are smart. The topic is still proper nouns and the specific subject for this round remains international rivers of the world. Students have to name any river outside of the United States to have a successful answer.

One of the fun things about the game is also how students have to ring in to answer the questions. Mrs. Grand gives each team a squeeze toy that lets out a sound when squeezed. The gold team has a rubber duck that lets out a loud "Quack" when a student squeezes it. This sound is the buzzer for the gold team. The red team has a rubber cow, and this rubber toy makes the sound of "Moo" when a student squeezes it. This sound is the buzzer for the red team.

Mrs. Grand repeats the question to the two girls asking them to name proper nouns that are international rivers of the world. Both girls are eagerly waiting to answer. Neeka immediately rings in first with a "quack" as she squeezes the rubber duckie that is used to indicate she has an answer. She squeezes it right before the "moo" of the red leader student Roxanne, so Neeka gets to answer first in her attempt at naming an international river of the world.

Neeka says, "The Nile River." The Nile River is a proper noun and an international river of the world. Mrs.

Grand confirms that she is correct. Now, Roxanne has to respond with a river of the world herself. If she can not respond with an answer right away, Mrs. Grand signals to begin the count, and in the next three seconds she has to say a correct answer or her team loses the point to the gold team.

Before the count is even signaled to begin, Roxanne says, "Amazon River."

All week long every time a student gets a correct answer during class or does exceptionally well on an assignment, Mrs. Grand puts a piece of candy in the bag o'candy. Mrs. Grand reminds the class, "Last Friday was an assembly day, and there was no Class-Wide Challenge game. This means there is now two weeks of candy to be won, and this is also the last day of school for the entire year, so I put an extra week of candy in the bag o' candy myself."

Three weeks of candy in one bag! Halloween in June! All the candy, with none of the cold and rain! "This gettin' good" says a student in a yellow top as he clenches the ends of his untucked shirt before he is corrected for his poor English grammar by Mrs. Grand.

Chapter 3

After five rounds of two very bright young students going back and forth, every single eyeball in the classroom is closing in on the two students working for the ultimate candy prize. From the mouth breathing computer gamers to the future reality show girls trying to pretend they don't care about the outcome and still look cute at the same time, no one moves. They all nervously stare intensely at the gold team's student, Neeka. Finally, after five rounds of correct answers, no answer comes immediately from Neeka this time when Mrs. Grand asks a knowledge question. The teacher holds up her hand signifying the red leaders can begin their count. If the opposing team reaches the count of three, the round will be over, and the red leaders will have won the point and tied up the game for the triple stuffed bag o' candy for this week's Class-Wide Challenge.

The whole class is excited. Michael Jefferson is staring at his teammate Neeka and starts to wince. He knows four or five more rivers, but he cannot answer because it is all up to Neeka. It is her turn. The other team begins the count with a controlled but slightly loud count of,

"Count ONE...," the situation does not look good for Neeka, Michael Jefferson, or his team of gold leaders...

"Count TWO..." comes the count from the red leader team,

"...Count THR–"

"The Yellow River," Neeka screams, and the counting stops with a disappointing moan from the red leaders as Mrs. Grand allows the last-second answer by Neeka.

"Whew." Michael Jefferson let out a big breath that he doesn't even know he is holding. The gold leaders hug and congratulate each other, and their mouths begin to salivate as the bag o'candy is soon to be theirs.

They all now quickly turn to stare down Roxanne, hoping to put the same intense pressure on her thoughts and block any rivers from coming into her mind through the psychic power of sugar craving grammar school students. Roxanne slowly blinks her oversized eyes at all of the students on both teams, and she moves her head left to right.

Then, before her count can even begin, she says with great confidence to the class, "The Rhine River." The red leaders are now slapping hands and doing an uncoordinated sloppy dance or two. The gold leaders, along with, and especially, Neeka, look entirely dejected.

Neeka knows that she mustered her very last answer with her Yellow River response during her last turn. After a moment the teacher motions for the red leaders to begin their count like an executioner motioning to a firing squad. The count comes quickly, Count- one, count- two, count-three. Neeka is silent. The red captain quickly and rather quietly, congratulates his team member, Roxanne. The class was taught that they can always loudly cheer when someone on their team gets an answer, but they can never loudly cheer when someone on the other team fails to answer, or they will lose the point themselves. Even with the low congratulations, the smiles begin to come across the red leaders faces, and Roxanne's eyes light up as she turns to her team as Mrs. Grand congratulates both young ladies on a well-played round. The red team has tied up the score just as the school day will soon come to an end.

Mrs. Grand, like most teachers, feels the best plan at this point is to evenly split the candy between both teams. With such a full bag o' candy this seems to be a good idea and a way for all students to head home for the summer with candy in their hands. But then the low voice of a student stands out. It is Timmy Manzo of the gold team. The little guy is small everywhere except just a bit over-grown in his waistline and just a bit over-excited about the bag o' candy and can't contain himself any longer. Like most students, he has been thinking about the bag o' candy since the beginning of the school day, which inspires Timmy to forcefully say, "There are no ties in grammar school! There are no ties for the last bag o' candy of the year!"

Members of the class respectfully agree with Timmy Manzo who stands proud like a newly elected senator. Then a very, very, confident young student named Brandrick of the red team speaks up in his calm, solid, and mature voice, and says, "Unless the gold team is scared or has no one to challenge me, I will gladly represent the red leaders in one final tie-breaker round question." The little boy in yellow once again blurts out, "This gettin' good." Then he quickly apologizes and corrects the grammatical error himself as he glances toward Mrs. Grand out of the corner of his eyes.

"This is getting to be a good competition among our intelligent classroom of young individuals" is the new line he comes up with as Mrs. Grand gives him a skeptical, blazing teacher look she has more than perfected by this point in the year.

Chapter 4

"I think I want to challenge Brain-rick, I mean Brandrick, Mrs. Grand," Michel Jefferson says as he inches forward and steps around Timmy Manzo to move in a bit from the outer circle that always forms during the weekly class challenge. Michael is looking at his team. Timmy Manzo nods his head up and down like a kung fu master saying, 'yes, you are ready young one— go forth and do well.' Other students on Michael's team are kind of shaking their heads the other way, back and forth in a no motion. The look on their faces is more of a look of 'oh, no, not again, not facing Brandrick. This is going to be a horrendous loss for sure.'

Brandrick is affectionately known as Brain-rick by his fellow students. He is a cool character in the classroom and cool to most other students in the classroom. Outside of a rather tall high-top fade haircut and circle glasses, Brain-rick blends into the class rather well, considering what he calls his advanced intelligence. Everyone likes him, and nobody likes him all at the same time because he shows some arrogance as a student when he gets his answers right during the week. But all of his correct answers also put a lot of sweets in the bag o'candy. Brain-rick is as much a positive acknowledgment by his classmates as it is teasing as well. Either name you call him, Brandrick, or Brain-rick, he is the smartest person in the class and likely the school for that matter. And he just issued a challenge to the gold leaders for the ultimate bag o' candy to end the school year.

Michael Jefferson is one of the best students on the gold leaders, but he isn't a straight "A" student and definitely isn't known as Brain-rick, but Neeka from the gold leaders has already recovered from her challenge loss against Roxanne and says with positivity, "Michael, you are great at geography. We want you to try to beat Brandrick." Neeka is being sure to use his real name in an attempt to lessen the emphasis on what must be his over-sized brain.

A tiebreaker happened once earlier this year, and Brain-rick obliterated his opponent to the point where he named eight additional answers he didn't even have to after winning the tie-breaking round.

Michael says, "Yes, I will represent the gold leaders."

Mrs. Grand sets up the next round, "Okay, boys, both of you inside the circle. The object is still proper nouns. Michael, take your duck. We will be listening for the quack. Brandrick, please take the toy cow from Roxanne, and we will listen for the moo. Are both of you ready?"

"Yes" and "yes" are the replies from Brain-rick and Michael in that order. Mrs. Grand then follows by repeating the question guidelines as if she is teaching a lesson. With all of the students so intently focused on the tie-breaker round, Mrs. Grand knows it is an opportune time to get one more drop of knowledge into their heads before the end of the school year.

Michael feels the intense pressure of the moment and thinks deeply to himself about this being the perfect time to fly away as he glances toward a cracked window, but thoughts of his team keep him locked into the center of the circle with the ultimate bag o' candy on the line. Having somewhat of a dramatic tone in her voice, Mrs. Grand continues to introduce the last round and says, "The topic is still proper nouns and, well then, you boys get ready to signal because here comes the specific subject."

The whole class tenses up for a moment as Mrs. Grand looks directly at Michael and Brain-rick and then says. "The specific subject is… international oceans and seas!" QUACKKKK–MOOOOO, Michael squeezes the duck so hard he thinks that the little toy eyes are going to pop out. Michael knows he gets in first, and so does the entire class; both teams are now staring at him. He easily says, "the Pacific Ocean," and is well on his way to the bag 'o candy. Brain-rick replies just as quickly, and even abruptly, "Atlantic!" he says with a quick start. All the known oceans are rapidly said. Now both students are left to call out the seas of the world. Brain-rick is able to rattle off the Red sea, Michael comes back with the Mediterranean Sea, Brain-rick says the Caribbean and South China, Michael hesitates slightly longer but does reply to both in turn with the Baltic and the Japan Sea. Back and forth, back and forth–even Mrs. Grand is amazed. Both students are now saying answers that Mrs. Grand hadn't even covered in this week's lessons.

Brain-rick then even seems to struggle a bit, to the point

that the count is about to begin. Still, he recovers from momentarily looking like an ordinary student who doesn't always have the answer at the very front of his mouth and says with a fair amount of confidence, "The Celtic sea, Mrs. Grand." "Ooooh!" goes the entire red leader team in unison. The gold leaders are grumbling and grinding their teeth as they see the candy slipping through their fingers into the hands of the other team.

Michael now realizes something. The pace of the game had been so fast, he'd just been reacting, but now he realizes he doesn't know any more seas. He tries to think back if one he knows hadn't been said. Then he thinks about the oceans. No, he remembers all of the oceans were said right away. Michael knows this is going to be a problem.

As Michael is finally going to collapse trying to come up with one more ocean or sea, he feels he is going to expire right in front of the class. Brain-rick, for the first time in his academic career, looks like he is rather unsure of himself as well. Mrs. Grand sensing the overall tension and fatigue of the two student participants calls the whole affair, "A testament to learning!" She adds that it has to be called, "A brilliant tie." But the moans from the students are quickly audible and loud. Half of the fun of winning the candy is smacking your lips full of chocolate and sugary treats right in front of the students who don't get any candy immediately after school.

Both teams look thoroughly disappointed in her temporary ruling. Timmy Manzo looks like he has two cotton balls in his mouth as his cheeks start to puff up and out with frustration. He has a personal disdain for ties the way most children despise broccoli. "Okay, Okay" Mrs. Grand says, "but this is the last turn for both; look at the clock. Do you want to stay here all summer just to see who claims the candy?" "Yes!" was the call from most of the students. But the cool looking future reality show girls say, "We have three stores and a nail appointment to get to. Do you think the candy can be dropped off at our houses if the gold team wins?"

Chapter 5

The school day and year are truly coming to an end. Looking at the clock, Mrs. Grand sees that in about five more minutes summer vacation will begin. There really is only time for one more round in this contest. This is going to have to be the last attempt for each student to answer. Mrs. Grand makes all of this very clear to even the most competitive and feisty students. She says to both students, "Here we go. The topic is still proper nouns, and the subject is still international oceans and seas. Michael, do you have any more to lend?"

Brain-rick, before the count is even signaled to begin for Michael, and even though it is not even officially his turn, says very stoically, "Mrs. Grand, at this time, I have no more answers to present. In order to preserve my exemplary scores this year, I will study more tonight. I can write a full report on all of the seas of the world, every last one of them, and then I will promptly email it to your posted school email account over the summ–"

"—No, no," Mrs. Grand interrupts, "your grade will

not be affected by this game, you have given us a number of great answers that would astonish a college professor, as always."

Then Mrs. Grand turns to Michael and says to him, "Michael, from the look on your face, I think you are out of responses as well. Do you have any more to lend, or shall we just call it a wondrous tie?" Nothing is heard, silence comes from Michael as a soft stare of confusion comes over his face.

Michael stands motionless peering toward the classroom doorway. He is glancing through the clear glass portion of the top half of the classroom door looking just outside of the glass into the hallway. It appears the pressure of the moment is finally getting to Michael who has been very composed and even heroic in the eyes of his team to this point. Now a frozen glance comes over his face as he continues to peer out into the hallway from where he stands. Mrs. Grand continues, "So it looks like we will call it a tie then." This is to be the final summary from Mrs. Grand. Both sides look dejected. It looks like no team will have any bragging rights for the entire bag o' candy on this day.

"Wait."

The word wait is heard throughout the classroom. The word comes from the grammar school student who thought he could fly. Michael Jefferson says it again, "WAIT." Every face turns, every eye focuses, some in disdain, others with great hope, Michael says, "I have one more."

Mrs. Grand, questioningly says with a raised pitch in her voice as she states his name, "Michael?"

Michael continues his glance outward from the group

of his classmates and is peering at the doorway to see a solitary child outside of the classroom. This little one outside of the class in the hallway is shorter and younger than the classmates in the room. She is bopping her head up and down, glancing back into the classroom at the Class-Wide Challenge proceedings.

Michael's soft gaze continues to focus on this small gnome like human being still bouncing her head up and over the lower portion of the wooden door to gain a look through the upper glass window into the classroom. Michael sees a brief flash of dark braided hair up and down, up and down, continue to peek in the window for the final few moments of the Class-Wide Challenge game. He sees a set of eyes that are happily glowing as they quickly appear and reappear as they rise high enough to look into the classroom window and then fall right below the window line on the classroom door.

Michael Jefferson, who thought he could fly, has one more answer to lend. He now turns his focus back to the class. For a moment Michael considers flying away as he feels the intense pressure of the entire room staring at him. He takes a quick, anxious breath of air through his nose, glances out at the window in the door, and clears his throat. Michael stops then starts and then begins– slightly soft spoken but definitely out loud so all can hear his final answer. He ultimately is able to say his two word answer, "Billy Ocean."

What ocean? A what...? The smart kids laugh at the oddity of the answer, immediately knowing that Michael can't be correct. The not so smart kids laugh trying to look like they know why everyone else is laughing. Mrs. Grand says, "Sorry, Michael, do you really have an answer? Let's start the count and make it official," she announces as she motions to the red leaders.

"Count one," they say.

"Wait a second," Michael says, still half quietly as he has a glazed look of semi-confusion on his face himself. Still, he is able to be a little louder and slightly more confident this time when he says, "Wait," audibly before his voice tails off, and he repeats, "Wait a second," more quietly and timidly while he takes another glance out of the classroom door. The small bouncing child in the window is still peeking in the classroom with every jump as energetic as the last. Michael takes a short breath and raises his finger to the sky and toward the dust covered vents in the classroom overhead like he has found some inspiration hiding in the poorly cleaned classroom ventilation system.

He gets Mrs. Grand's attention further by changing his raised finger to a slight questioning finger wave in front of his own face. He does this to alert Mrs. Grand that he is seriously answering her question as he speaks the two words, "Billy Ocean," again.

Mrs. Grand stops the count by waving her own hands above her head. Michael takes this moment to jump in and clearly explain as best he can with a lump of tightness in his throat, "You said we were naming proper nouns, then you said the subject was international oceans and seas." Michael continued, now speaking to Mrs. Grand directly, but speaking quietly as if he is gently waking her from a mid-day meditation. "Billy Ocean is a proper noun. He is a singer; it isn't a made-up answer. He's a singer, and a proper noun and…" The class crowd is not laughing and is now just puzzled and making odd, confused noises and faces at Michael and each other. Michael Jefferson not only thought he could fly, he thought he could win the biggest bag o' candy of the year with his strange new answer.

Now, Billy Ocean is a singer who has a number of "oldie hits," and he is technically from outside of the United States and international, or "of the world," and Mrs. Grand is a teacher who is an "oldie" herself when compared to a grammar school student. She does know the musical artist and remembers a couple of his songs, but how can she allow the answer, Billy Ocean? She deliberates, then reviews the criteria of her original question in her mind and reviews her entire lesson for the week on proper nouns and international oceans and seas of the world.

She contemplates exactly how she had phrased her question and seems stumped a bit herself. She reviews in her mind that she hasn't said bodies of water. Mrs. Grand cringes, furrows her brow, twists her scarf, looks down at the golden apple pin on her neatly pressed blazer covering her clean tucked in blouse. She turns to the grammar poster on the wall defining a proper noun. Mrs. Grand looks up and directly at the politician-to-be Timmy Manzo who is staring her down like he just asked her a direct question in a nationally televised debate. She thinks the answer, Billy Ocean, to be outrageous, unlikely, creative, confusing, bold, and coming from a young child quite kooky. And in the end, she throws up her hands part in discovery, part in acknowledgment, part in disdain, and part out of respect for the ingenuity and does allow the answer, Billy Ocean!

The red team slumps over the surrounding desks, chairs, and even to the floor in disbelief. The gold team

even more in disbelief, most of them still not truly under-
standing what happened, plunge their hands deep into the
three times full bag o'candy and start to smack their lips at
the other team just as the final school bell of the year rings
with a loud and long shrill ring.

The little boy in yellow from the red team is pounding
his fists and even his forehead on the desk, part angry, part
exhausted, but mostly confused, saying over and over again,
"This no good, this no good," as proper grammar was the
least of his concern at this point. And he continues, "This
no good, this no good at all, this no good for the last day of
school, this no good for humanity, this no good for children's emotions." Michael and the gold leaders continue to
dive into the ultimate bag o' candy and race to the door to
begin their summer vacation as Mrs. Grand is issuing
condolences and congratulations to the students and
mentioning all the books they are to read over the summer.

Chapter 6

Michael makes it to the classroom door with a few general nods from some of his classmates and some quick congratulations from Neeka and a few others. Most of the students are definitely more worried about summer vacation and the candy in hand than any sort of group celebration.

At the door, the solitary jumping figure is now right next to Michael, still bopping up and down. She meets him at the classroom door as he crosses into the hallway. They both walk down the short hallway side-by-side toward the school exit doors. Michael had poured a good portion of the bag o' candy into his own backpack, but still has two full hands of candy as he is attempting to zip it up. The small figure is more bouncing up and down than walking, even though there is no longer a window to peek into. She begins to pick at the oversized double hand full of candy that Michael is spilling from his hands into his backpack. She is intercepting a few pieces during the transfer. With her energy, candy seems to be one of the last things she needs.

The young student who followed the game and mass excitement looking in the window through most of the last round is T.J. She is Michael's cousin and is two grades younger than Michael. Whenever T.J. completes an entire week without being "squirrely," which is about once every three or four weeks, she is allowed to leave class ten minutes early on Friday and look in on Mrs. Grand's class.

At first, when she was lucky, she even got to see a minute or two of the Class-wide challenge game while sitting inside Mrs. Grand's class. Due to her ample cheers, Hollywood studio like applause, moans, golf claps, and general exaggerated facial expressions with each answer, she is no longer allowed in the actual classroom. But as long as she is quiet in the hall, she can watch from the hallway when they are playing the game, so she can meet Michael right at the classroom door when the bell rings. Normally, T.J. stands on a couple of her books and then on her tiptoes to just barely be able to see into the classroom. Today being the last day of school T.J. has no books and only a couple of loose papers to bring home. She threw most of the papers away in the hallway trash can walking to Michael's classroom anyway.

She has an empty backpack except for a music player she keeps in the interior hidden backpack pocket. She gains just as much joy from being able to hop up and down and see from outside of the classroom as she does being inside. She saw it was a wild game and could see the expressions on the students' faces with every correct and incorrect answer.

Even more importantly for T.J. is being able to meet Michael right when he leaves the class at the doorway to start their weekend together. She is much more well behaved when she is around Michael. T.J. idolizes her cousin who is almost a full two years older than she is.

After picking through a handful of the candy that T.J. has on display in the palm of her left hand, T.J. begins to dig into the backpack for a few more select pieces. She immediately sees two of her favorite types of candies sitting back to back and looks up at Michael like he has delivered her two winning lottery tickets. She begins to break into her first type of laugh. T.J. has a few different laughs; this one is a sly smile and funny giggle that she makes when she is overjoyed and happy. She giggles as she is grabbing her favorite candies and slyly smiles.

Chapter 7

T.J. is still bouncing up and down as she simultaneously speaks and enjoys her first few chews of candy, "That was a big bag of candy this time. We should store some in our cheeks like chipmunks." T.J. looks up at Michael with the two favorite pieces of candy now wedged in her cheeks and gives a full grin, "Thanks for winning my favorites," she says to Michael in a garble but still understandable manner.

Michael says, "It was you who gave me the final answer." Michael continues, "I used your musical knowledge to win."

T.J. says, "Oh, it was a singing game this week. Awesome. Did you sing? Did you sing?" Oh that's awesome. I'm going to sing…"

"No, I used an answer," Michael interrupted before T.J. bursts into song before they are outside the school building. T.J. was banned from singing in the school building earlier in the year and has done pretty well in keeping her singing under her breath and keeping herself in humming mode inside the building most of the year.

"There was no singing, but you used my singing to win? How did that work?" T.J. asks. Michael continues, "Well, it is hard to explain, but the winning answer was Billy Ocean."

T.J. repeats the answer. "Billy Ocean for the candy. You went to Billy Ocean for the biggest bag o' candy of all time. Amazing." As T.J. pops a piece of candy in her mouth just as she finishes the previous two pieces, the cousins reach outside of the school building and are more than halfway across the short playground to leave the school grounds. T.J., as clearly as possible while chewing on a piece of soft candy, breaks into a verse from Billy Ocean's song, "When the Going Gets Tough, the Tough Get Going." In T.J.'s mind, whenever she sings she thinks of her song list and the ratings in her personal journal/notebook. She reviews her written notes every night before she goes to sleep.

T.J.'s Song List and Ratings:

When the Going Gets Tough, the Tough Get Going

- Music : 4 and 1/2 stars
- Singer: 5 stars
- Mom Meaning: <u>Inspirational</u>. You can do it! Keep trying! - I can hear mom saying that.

The singing is stopped by Michael, when he says, "T.J., you're going to choke while singing best of the 80's music." T.J. continues to move a couple more pieces of candy around in her mouth as she stops singing to eat a few more brightly colored candies. The older protective cousin is both making sure T.J. doesn't choke and making sure she doesn't get hit by a car. He is watching the crosswalk as they quickly cross one of the two major streets on their walk home before they reach the block where their house is.

T.J. moves to her humming tone now that she has a good number of pieces of candy and is momentarily unable to actually sing words. She is genuinely interested in what Michael does at most times, and as she finishes off a few more chews of the massive amount of candy in her mouth, she is able to ask Michael to explain how he used Billy Ocean to win the ultimate bag o' candy.

Michael looks down at T.J. and begins to animate his voice, "Story time," he says as he looks like he is ready to take flight and leap into the sky.

Michael going into "story time" about his day at school is the greatest way to get T.J. to have a good night at home. He often refers to the story he tells on the way home or even re-tells it entirely, if requested, when the two cousins are at home in the evening and T.J. feels the need to be with Michael. Michael always tries his best to recapture what- ever big moment of the day happened when he explains his life in detail to T.J. on their daily walks home from school.

Michael quickly gets deep into the story and tells T.J. with great suspense how he stared down Brain-rick, the boy with a supercomputer for a brain! He continues scribing how he went round for round and saw smoke coming out of the computer's brain because he was making the circuits and memory chips and motherboard work so hard. He says, "I even heard either the computerized boy's auxiliary fan cut on to super-drive so the unit wouldn't overheat! It was either the auxiliary fan or a grammar school child passing gas from all of the tension built up watching the titanic competition."

T.J. interrupted the story with a long blender laugh. It is a glorious outburst. That is T.J.'s second type of many laughs. It arrives as a triumphant sound that seems to occur when she thinks something is hilarious, often only to her. It is known as her blender laugh. It can only be described as a blender laugh, as T.J. revs up her laughter to a churning sound that makes you think someone is making a light smoothie somewhere nearby. The laughter sounds rise up and down like a pulsating blender. It is heard through the street as they are walking and coming close to home, "ErrrHa-rararara, ErrrHa-rararara, ErrrHa-rararara."

After the blender laugh calms down, Michael brings T.J. into the story with more narration, saying a tear came into flying Michael's eye as he thought he was going to lose the bag o' candy for his team. He was out of answers, and it was his turn. The computerized brain boy was mechanically staring at him. But then his super cousin, due to her good behavior, was released early from the claws of the lower grade evil teacher and was jumping up and down to send the answer telepathically just in time to her cousin, Michael. She saved the bag o' candy then heard thunderous applause when they won." Michael says, "You heard and saw the rest of the story." This is T.J.'s favorite part of the day, the walk home with her older cousin, hearing the wondrous stories from the upper grades of their school. This is the only real fun that T.J. has throughout the day this last year since the tough losses in their family, including T.J.'s mother. When it is story time late at night, her mother used to tell crazy funny stories about running around in "Purple Rain" or action adventures in some far away "Danger Zone" based on old songs T.J. listened to with her mom.

Michael isn't able to create the funny scenarios and story titles of T.J.'s mother during the simple walk home, but it is quickly seen why T.J. is so close to and looks up to her cousin. As he is speaking to her and placing her in the story, it is the first time she becomes calm since her bouncing up and down at the window. She is not bouncing up and down. She is not singing or humming. She is walking by Michael's side on the last day of school next to her protector and friend, involved in every word of what he is saying. All of this ends when Michael finishes re-telling the tale of how he won the ultimate bag o'candy with a glorious outburst of another blender laugh. "ErrrHa-rararara, ErrrHa-rararara, ErrrHa-rararara" is heard up and down the street as they walk and come closer together playfully bumping into each other as the best friends and cousins reach the block of their home.

Part II

M ichael and T.J.'s house fits into their neighborhood as best it can. The house definitely has its own unique "upgrades" as Michael's mother calls them. It is a medium to small size home with horizontal wood planks across most of the front with an odd patch of wood shingles covering a small part of the front of the home. The wood shingles continue from the odd patch in front to covering the side and back. The house is a mix of a blue/tan color. Some smaller sections of the horizontal wood are colored solid blue, and a few other boards are tan.

If someone asked a home designer what the color of the house is, they would look puzzled and say blue with tan accents, or tan with blue accents or just call it bland because in some places the blue and tan run together. Michael and T.J. have a lot of jokes about the look of the house. When anyone asks T.J. what color the house is, she always says, "confused color" matter-of-factly like it is one of the primary colors.

The cousins reach the small area that is the front yard

and walk the few paces up to the three stairs leading onto the small porch and into the house. Michael pulls out seven more pieces of candy and says to T.J., "Put the candy in your pocket because we both know 'AuntMom' is going to take this bag as soon as we walk into the house."

T.J. gets a quick last word in and says, "Hide the candy in our cheeks, I tell ya, just like chipmunks" as she plants one more full piece of candy in her mouth, gives a chipmunk like grin, and has a last giggling fit for Michael before they reach the inside of their home.

She puts the pieces of candy Michael gave her into her pocket, picks a few more of her favorites from Michael's backpack and begins to hide those as well. Michael's mom is there to greet them only a few steps inside the door. She tells them to get to the kitchen and unload all their school stuff from their backpacks on the kitchen table because they will need the bags for their trip on Sunday. Michael's mother is T.J.'s aunt, and as they live together they both almost always refer to her as "AuntMom," pronounced AntMom.

T.J. convinces Michael's mom that AuntMom sounds cool. It is almost like Ant-Man which is one of the favorite comic books T.J. takes from Michael's small collection of comics every so often. She likes looking at the colorful pictures while she listens to her music more than reading the actual comic stories. The Ant-Man drawings are some of her favorites. T.J. likes how being the little guy seems to be a way that Ant-Man works out a lot of problems in the end.

The unloading of the backpacks on the kitchen table leaves plenty of exposed candy. AuntMom quickly looks at

T.J. and says, "I hope you don't plan on having any more of that tonight. You will be bouncing off the walls more than usual." T.J. looks directly at AuntMom with cheeks overflowing with candy and says in a garbled voice, "No, I'm good here," as she snatches a paper towel off of the countertop and dashes around the corner. She quietly pulls a few pieces of candy out of her mouth and tucks them away in the paper towel to save for later. A faint garbled blender laugh, ErHa-rararara, is heard as T.J. ascends up the stairs to her bedroom to listen to her music player.

T.J.'s room is a bit odd, like most of the family home. From the outside it looks like a small two-story home. Inside it is more of a one and a half story home with three rooms occupying a space above the larger than expected ground floor. The ground floor has four good sized rooms. There is a kitchen with an eating area large enough for a table and six chairs. The downstairs also has a living room and a dining room that has not been used for eating in over a year, so now it is more of an overcrowded office and has a few extra pieces of furniture in it. The fourth room is a slightly above average sized bathroom with a sink, toilet, and small bathtub.

Back on the upper floor is a smaller bathroom with an even smaller shower. One of the two upstairs rooms is further divided by plywood to give Michael and T.J. their own rooms. Although T.J. speaks to Michael through the plywood constantly as if they are sitting side by side in the same room. Michael's mom, T.J.'s aunt, sleeps upstairs in the other room that is nearby Michael and T.J.'s split situation, but not right next to them. The room is on the other side of the small bathroom. AuntMom keeps most of her clothes in a wardrobe downstairs just around the corner from the bigger downstairs bathroom. The downstairs bathroom has a tiny bathtub that AuntMom treats like a luxury spa retreat when she has a chance to use it. She likes having her clothes nearby.

The house has no basement that you would spend much time in. There is a cellar or an "underneath" as Michael and T.J. call it. It has a lot of old relics down there and serves as an occasional pantry for a few items. The Jefferson family rarely has what can be called surplus of anything, but when they do, they utilize the underneath for pantry space. When not called the underneath, it is occasionally referred to by Michael and T.J. as the next world war bomb shelter whenever 0-80 isn't around to hear the reference to war.

Chapter 9

AuntMom is speaking to Michael about his school day while he is pulling a few summer assignments he has from his teachers out of his bag. He continues to pick at the candy as his mom says, "You can take the candy with you." She adds, "you can take it on vacation, but for now, tell me more about your summer assignments."

Her motherly ways continue as they always do for the first twenty minutes that Michael is home from school. "Take your shoes and T.J.'s bag and put them in the corner." AuntMom scoops up the candy and puts half of it in a plastic bag, and the other half she sneakily throws away under the top layer of trash in the kitchen trashcan next to the counter space.

As she finds another spare moment, she moves the rest of the candy into the freezer inside the big empty box labeled frozen brussel sprouts. This is the surest way to keep the candy out of Michael's and T.J.'s hands, but especially T.J. For now the rest of the bag of candy is on top of the microwave that sits on the kitchen counter. AuntMom reminds Michael to make sure T.J. does not touch another piece until Sunday afternoon when they get out of the car at the campsite.

"I want you to save any and all hyperactivity for Sunday when you are in the great outdoors where all of nature can try to contain Miss T.J."

Upstairs T.J., with earbuds already in, is listening to music and doesn't hear any of what AuntMom says. Even if she were downstairs and nearby, T.J. has mastered the art of being nearby physically while being distant and off someplace far away in her mind with her music and her headphones on or earbuds in. AuntMom says, "Michael, fly around all you want for about an hour but be back in this room by dinnertime."

Going out to see 0-80's place is actually just walking out of the side door of the house leading from the kitchen over about five feet of chipped concrete to the garage that is converted to an apartment like space for 0-80. When Michael steps inside and sees O-80's garage room, he is always surprised at how semi-dark 0-80 keeps the space, even in the daytime.

This garage has one truly full–sized window across from the side door that Michael walks in. It has a smaller window on the door that is now right behind Michael as he walks fully into the garage apartment. Somewhat surprisingly, it has a slender skylight off center toward the front of the roofline that leaves an interesting beam of light cutting through the space. Each of these sources give off reduced light due to the yellow construction paper covering part of the windows. 'Privacy glass' is what 0-80 calls it. Even in low light, you can still see a unique style of wallpaper spread across the back and side wall of the garage that gives the entire space a wondrous feel.

The wallpaper Michael is looking at on the far wall is a complete line of maps. They cover the back wall from floor to near the ceiling. They are from Europe, Asia, Africa, North America, South America, and beyond, including seas and bodies of water. All of the days and hours spent in the dark space with 0-80 staring at the wallpaper that are actually maps definitely helped Michael take down Brain-rick in school earlier that day.

The space was at one point a two car garage and has a very high ceiling to be a garage. The high ceilings were great for storage at some point. The height is now being used in an even better way as it creates an amazing loft space where 0-80 has a single twin bed and a very large hammock. He also has a drafting table being used as a desk in the loft space. 0-80 sits at the desk at the moment. He spends most of his time up above in the loft space in what the family calls the "garage apartment."

Below the loft space is a couch, both old and uncomfortable. It is facing a TV and a couple of other old basic wooden chairs that look like they are embarrassed to not be refinished at this stage in their lives. The walls and roof were insulated when the garage became an apartment to make it more livable and warm. The floor is concrete with a patch of rug here and there, but mostly cool concrete.

In the loft area is exactly where Michael expects to find 0-80 as he fully enters the garage apartment and stands in the center of the room. He takes a step toward the loft, pounding down on the concrete, expecting to lift himself up in flight. His chest raises up to be strong and cut through the air. In his mind he expects to land up in the loft next to 0-80 near the oversized hammock.

Michael doesn't take flight, so he settles for the cool looking rolling ladder. It is a ladder a college professor might use in an old library to get dusty books off of the top shelf while looking for a specific book on extinct butterfly types or ancient Egyptian symbols. The type of book that is only found with one of those rolling ladders.

Michael makes his way up the seven steps of the ladder. He is always amazed when he reaches step four and his eye line reaches sight of the loft. Looking up in the space with all of the maps looking back at him makes the loft area that 0-80 has created a unique, mysterious, murky, and alluring place. The ladder itself does not roll across the floor. 0-80 fastens it to the near side of the garage closest to the door because he says, in his condition with his old creaking bones, it is hard enough to climb up a regular ladder, let alone one that might roll across the room with you on it. "I can't just jump on some broom from those Harry Wizard movies you kids are always trying to get me to watch," is 0-80's go-to line when they ask to unhook the ladder so they can roll it across the garage like a type of roller coaster ride.

Once at the top of the library-like ladder, one could see there is no bookshelf in the loft area, but there are a number of books stacked up in three or four different vertical stacks on the side of the room with the drafting table. Upon inspection, the books are actually a lot of world atlas type of books, or they aren't books at all. They are just maps. As it turns out, the lower portion of the garage maps on the back and side wall are just some of the additional maps that won't fit in the loft area. The loft space itself is covered end to end and even on the ceiling. The ceiling has a gradual angle to the center point of the room. Every inch is covered by maps.

Chapter 10

When Michael reaches the top of the ladder, he walks into the loft space with its smooth wood floors. There are a few other items around the room that makes the space even more intriguing to a curious and studious middle school student like Michael. There is a compass sitting on the drafting table near where 0-80 currently sits. A flashlight is standing up vertically next to the bed, and a lot of military gadgets or gear look like they were hurriedly displayed as they sit off in three of the four corners of the room.

Michael goes to the oversized hammock and leans down into it. Swinging back and forth slightly while staring up at the ceiling of maps, it even looks and feels like you are traveling from island to island. Moving land to land across the oceans and seas is the immediate feeling as Michael looks up at a large map of what was primarily the lands of Western Asia and sways back and forth. Michael's win for the ultimate bag o'candy has to give credit to the loft set up and swaying back and forth on the hammock looking at 0-

80's maps for days on end in the slightly darkened space that unknowingly makes you focus intensely to see the places on each map.

After saying "Hi," to 0-80, which is returned with a nod from 0-80 but no audible reply, Michael leans forward in the hammock and glances at a map on the wall that is near 0-80's twin bed and says, "The Caspian Sea helped get candy for my class and me today." 0-80 snaps back like a tired old man, "Well, the Caspian Sea got me a bunch of wet underwear and smelly socks for two months and a half. It is no fun out in the field, I tell ya."

0-80 rarely lets a chance go when he can remind anyone who will listen to him about his broken down body and aged spirit and mind. He does have a dash of prema-ture grey on the side of his almost feathered but mostly curly hair, but it does little to make him look a day over twenty-nine, let alone like an old, old, old, old, old, old, old, old, old man.

0-80's mind goes pop, pop, pop like a bug zapper working around a picnic table at a summer family reunion. Memories, both good and bad flash into his mind.

He stands slowly and abruptly and says suddenly and way too loud. "The last map! It is right in the area of the last map!"

0-80 speaks like a person trying to get someone's atten-tion in a movie theater. Not too loud, but still way too loud. Then his voice trails off into the nearby dust in the room.

Despite a few outbursts like this one, Michael likes to study in 0-80's room. It is a great study area because his uncle pretty much demands a library-like environment at all times from everyone but himself when they come into his garage apartment. The only regular exceptions are if he is watching some type of sports. Then it is okay to be moderately animated if it is late in a game, like the fourth quarter of a playoff game or something.

It is this same library type environment that discourages T.J. to go out to see her dad, 0-80, too often. T.J. is always singing and flopping around to music to keep her mind on her mom. 0-80 is always trying to get time to stop right where it is and then slowly wind each day back until he goes back far enough to bring T.J.'s mom back. Back when his only real goal in life was to come home and see T.J. with her mom, both of them smiling waiting for him, the heroic father and husband to return.

For Michael, time seems different in 0-80's garage. Michael easily wanders off and is at one of the places on the map and often has an hour or two go by. He thinks about shooting up into the sky and flying off to an island or tropical destination as his mind scans over the maps and locations that jump off the wall when he walks around the space during his almost daily visits to 0-80's garage apartment.

Just then, Michael realizes that he is supposed to be bringing 0-80 into the house for dinner, not getting lost in time and the walls of maps in 0-80's place. With that thought, the next sound that Michael hears is his mom telling both of them to come inside for dinner and to wash their hands.

The only bathroom is on the ground floor. It has a narrow stand up shower that also has a side seat that can be utilized when showering. It has a small sink and a toilet with a cushioned seat. Michael partly slides down the ladder and then jumps from the fourth step expecting to fly toward the bathroom. It appears he does for a brief moment, by jumping high in the air from the step, but he quickly and smoothly comes down to the floor and jogs to the back corner to wash his hands. 0-80 grumbles something about flying around and then slowly, very slowly, makes his way down the ladder as Michael has already washed his hands and jogs past 0-80 toward the side door to go to the kitchen in the house. 0-80 is somewhere shuffling like an old man behind him warning him not to jump one inch higher than a deck of playing cards.

Chapter 11

T.J. sits at the dinner table with a savory grin on her face and knife and fork in hand. She says a quick and quiet, "Hi Dad," and 0-80 tries to smile in return. Then, before AuntMom or 0-80 can say it, T.J. says, "No singing at the table," to remind herself not to burst into song while chewing on the mashed potatoes and macaroni cheese mix. It is her and Michael's favorite that they like to call MP and MMC. Mashed Potatoes and Mashed Macaroni and Cheese! Just as good as it sounds with all of the ingredients in the same large size spaghetti bowl mashed together for the main course of the family dinner.

This is to be a fun meal for the last day of school. The perfect celebration meal for a very imperfect year for T.J., Michael, and family. "Pass the MP and MMC, please," Michael says to T.J. as she is putting a third heaping pile on her plate. She looks up at Michael like he has interrupted her during heart surgery. She plops the third scoop on her plate to make a true mini pile of food that she begins to attack from the top down.

Michael also decides to begin the meal with a full three scoops but has evenly spread the MP and MMC across his plate. 0-80 and AuntMom have some of the same. They also have a protein shake of some kind along with the meal as well.

The discussion about school and the last day is a very brief one. With this year now officially behind them, neither Michael or T.J. see any need to speak further about it as a whole. AuntMom is more excited to talk about the future as well, and immediately her face lights up when she says, "You know that it is vacation time. You will have one day of rest here, and then on Sunday we are off to a special vacation for the first part of the summer."

Michael kind of groans a little. The family vacation every summer consists of a road trip of some type that ends with a hot day in the desert, camping trip, or some type of trip to the ski mountains during the summer months. The summertime—when no snow is to be seen for skiing, snowboarding, sledding, or even making a snowman. "Affordable off-season," is what AuntMom says. "We get to stay in a beautiful cabin, not a tent," she always says, "on the beautiful mountain, not a crowd in sight," she always says.

"A trip to a mountain with no snow!" Is what Michael usually grumbles back as he thinks about how he would have to pile into the backseat of the family car for the long road trip. Any trip more than an hour away is a guaranteed misadventure when all four remaining members of the family are in the car together, and Michael knows the journey to the mountains is hours away.

This year is to be different. AuntMom begins to explain, "This year isn't going to be the exact family vacation as years past. This year we are going to drop you and T.J. off at camp for two whole weeks of fun. There will be all types of fun activities for the both of you. To start, there will be zip-lining, which is a lot like flying, Michael."

Could be cool, but also seems a bit insulting to a boy who can fly, Michael thinks as he takes another big bite of his Mashed Potatoes and Mashed Macaroni and Cheese.

AuntMom continues, looking at both T.J. and Michael. "Making pottery, a lot of great hiking," she turns to T.J., "there will be plenty of campfire singing and making s'mores…"

Michael really does start to get excited about the summer vacation trip this year. AuntMom finishes her sales pitch saying, "…with such a long year, Michael, you have been supportive of the family and especially with T.J. at school." AuntMom says to both, "You and T.J. deserve to go off to the mountains and camp with a group. Everyone can run around as wild as they want to be," as she glances at T.J. "You both are finally old enough and responsible enough to do so."

T.J. says, "Me, wild? In the wild? With wildlife?" T.J. is very proud of her sentence and punctuated it with a short blender laugh Errr-Ha-Errr-Ha, just as AuntMom is saying, "Don't forget about wildflowers."

T.J. stops laughing and has a questioning look on her face as she has been out-shined by AuntMom's quick comment about wildflowers. She continues speaking about the wildflowers, saying, "They are beautiful up high in the mountains where you will be." AuntMom even promises it is even possible to see snow in June at the high levels they would be going to near the Big Mountain. They would see snow on the mountain tops even if it didn't reach their feet at their camp.

Michael is excited enough by the prospect of seeing snow, as he always thinks of flying up high into the sky and floating back to earth with a soft landing like a snowflake. Even better for Michael, he thinks about flying up into the sky and landing right in the middle of a pile of soft fluffy snow. 0-80 chimes in for the first time during the dinner conversation by going through a list of mountain ranges and heights that will be within a few hundred miles of Michael and T.J.'S campsite. He rattles off a number of locations and heights, including peak heights of 8,839 feet and 13,120 feet that are listed on the maps and atlases that he has.

0-80 says to Michael, "Do you remember seeing those in the atlas and topography maps?"

Michael says, "Yes, of course."

0-80 continues, "Those are some very special places. You should have a good time there." 0-80 has an almost pleased look on his face and a wrinkled smile that brightens his old man persona. Although Michael gets excited to go and already considers the leaps and bounds he will be able to take as he vaults into the sky while up in the outdoors park he still is not looking forward to the car ride to get there.

Chapter 12

When Sunday comes, the family piles into their car. Michael brightens his thoughts and is beginning to convince himself that the ride may be relatively dull. He has a few maps in hand and a comic book to keep him occupied. 0-80 is in his usual old and distant, disgruntled state. T.J. plugs into her music earbuds to mouth words all the way there. She isn't allowed to sing in the car. When the family goes on a long ride, this is usually how it starts. After about fifty minutes, like an alarm clock going off, each member of the family begins the misadventure in their own way.

As always, at the start of the trip, everything is pretty smooth. There is only one moment when AuntMom has to intervene. It is when Michael pulls out and fully unfolds one of his bigger maps, "accidentally" playfully smacking T.J. in the face a couple of times while they sit in the back seat together. A simple, "That's enough map acrobatics, Michael," is all it takes from AuntMom to keep the smooth start intact. Michael is looking at his maps, trying to out navigate the car's GPS, as they begin to leave familiar territory beyond their neighborhood and city.

This action of Michael trying to outwit the GPS now causes more than an occasional word by 0-80 as he begins by saying, "It is good of you to pull that map out, young fella'. A map never runs out of a battery, never talks back by constantly saying 're-routing', 're-routing', 're-routing'."

0-80 is now warmed up and ready to go on an "old man" rant. He claims loudly like he is trying to talk to someone who is outside of the car by nearly shouting, "When I learned how to drive, people were smart enough to look at the road they were driving on not look at a picture of the road they were driving on by staring at a dashboard computer." 0-80 isn't done, "I tell you, we didn't have heated seats. If you wanted a hot behind you put on long underwear before you got in the car."

Michael is able to drift out of the shouting conversation by thinking about how great it would be to leap into the sky and fly to all of the wonderful places he sees on the map. Michael's real excitement is over an old map he has tucked away in his bag. His mind races back twenty-four hours to a map he and 0-80 found at the library antique room in the special collections.

One day earlier, 0-80 spoke to Michael staring at a map in his garage apartment, "I figured something out when I was studying and thinking about the area where you and T.J. will be going to camp."

It was something he hadn't thought about in so long he wasn't sure.

"A trip to the library is necessary. Going out in the field."

Michael and 0-80 search in the library all day Saturday before the trip. They are not allowed to take maps out of special collections. But Michael shows 0-80 how to take pictures of some interesting maps with his phone. They both think it might kind of be against library rules, but Michael takes really good images. This causes even 0-80 to acknowledge the usefulness of a smartphone and say, "Hey, pretty good tech, Michael."

"The tech is only as smart as the person using it," Michael says, trying to cut off 0-80 before he has something else to say in one of his famous rants against the latest technology. Michael is too late.

"A smart phone in dumb hands makes dumb decisions every time. You kids need to learn that." 0-80 is talking to the phone itself now. "A phone can't be smart if the person holding it is as dumb as a rock; you remember that young fella." Michael gets the conversation back on track by looking at and talking to the phone as well, "Don't listen to him, you took great pictures, he even admitted it."

0-80 looks confused and scared now, "Don't tell me the thing has feelings you have to look after now, too! What will they think of next? Those are really good pictures though."

They immediately take the pictures of the maps back to 0-80's garage apartment. They print copies and add one to the "special collections" wallpaper section of 0-80's garage apartment wall. The other copy Michael holds onto to bring with him on the trip.

The map they came away with covers many years of trails and areas that aren't included on newer maps. New stations are built and upgraded, and land masses shift and so on. It is interesting how many people don't realize almost as soon as a map is created, even something as current as an online map, items can change or shift or adjust almost instantaneously. Michael admitted to 0-80, "In this way, maps are kind of like phones, often outdated upon completion."

The long trip looking at maps on Saturday confirmed what 0-80 had connected to the night before in his garage apartment. That connection led 0-80 to an old small trunk down in the cellar, or "the underneath" of the family home. All of 0-80's maps are in his apartment garage except for a small trunk just a little bigger than a tackle box. O-80 had one of the actual old antique maps they took a picture of at the library. He has the same map, or a very similar one given to him by his grandfather, Michael's great-grandfather. He retrieved the map late on Saturday night, along with a few other things from the small trunk, and put them in his travel bag for the trip.

Thinking about their Saturday together, Michael is reminded of the most fun parts about analyzing maps with 0-80. They both like to look at the changes over time. Michael then jokes with 0-80 and says to him in the front seat, "0-80, you're as old as Bombay", with a laugh as the word "Bombay" is always a funny city name from an old map that had been updated some years ago. 0-80 replies that he has maps with funnier names than that, "How do you like Crapstone, England? Or Santa Claus, Georgia?"

Both 0-80 and Michael share in the map humor while the rest of the family thinks they are just making up names.

T.J. is still mouthing away words to a song but is looking more and more restless by the minute. She's looking a bit distressed as she glances out the window at the highway racing by. T.J. isn't one to get carsick, but it looks like she is beyond anxious and maybe getting a bit of a fever as she squirms in her seat, and she places her hand over her mouth suddenly. Seeing this, along with AuntMom having heard about enough of 0-80's rants, the family pulls over at the next exit and decides to stop for burgers to make the whole trip better.

The first stop of the day! O-80 is sure T.J. has to burst out of the car to use the bathroom. The old timer hustles up to get the door unlocked and help T.J. unbuckle from her car seat. Just as he reaches T.J.'s car door, she bursts out of the car and jumps on the pavement and simultaneously hits the chorus, with her earbuds still in to Life is a Highway.

It is clear now that T.J.'s only issue was not being able to hold back singing a song from her music player that perfectly matches the family traveling down the open highway. There is no real emergency restroom need. Still T.J. is shuffling across the parking lot toward the small set of stores that includes a restroom, fast food restaurant, gas station, and small shop.

Michael also makes his way out of the car and takes a leap off the back car bumper and lifts off incredibly high, but falls short of what one would actually call flying as he hurries along a few paces to catch up with T.J. She is completing the last chorus as she walks and skips across to the Burger Shack parking lot.

T.J. says to Michael, "Almost couldn't hold that song in, one of Mom's favorites. I have been doing so good today." T.J. decides to punctuate the chorus one more time as a stranger passes by and says to T.J., "Hey, wasn't that the song from the Cars movie?" T.J. responds in her childlike tone, but with some authority and says, "Hey, no, Tom Cochrane 'Tom Cochrane-Cars movie remake,' that's what my mom's playlist says, and my mom was always right about music. My playlist is right, too."

T.J.'s song list and ratings:

Life is a Highway

- Music 5 stars
- Singer: 4 stars
- Mom Meaning: Don't stay in one place. Go find some adventure. Put down the phones. Come outside with your mom and dad. - I can hear mom saying that.

The stranger turns and says, "Okay, I heard it in a Cars movie before." T.J. slightly scoffs and goes from music mode to food mode as she looks up at the tall counter waiting to order her favorite burger.

Chapter 13

As they eat burgers, they all comment on how good the food is. "Almost as good as Happy's," Michael decides as he takes another handful of french fries from the french fry basket they are sharing. It is a rare treat that Michael and T.J. get to eat fast food, so the meal is rather uneventful. There isn't much talking outside of T.J. discussing her theory that little kids should always get two milkshakes and not just one.

"Milk is an essential building block for growing up and getting bigger."

Her theory does not result in T.J. getting an extra milk-shake, as AuntMom replies, "Vegetables are pretty essential too, but you aren't asking for a double supply of kale when I offer you some of my kale smoothie. It is just like a shake!" "Hey, no way," T.J. says, "a shake with kale. That is not a shake; kale rhymes with stale. I don't think it's good to eat stale anything."

AuntMom doesn't let her kale drink go undefended, when she says, "Well, shake rhymes with stomachache, that is why one is more than enough, and you aren't taking anything with you in the car, so hurry and finish your food."

T.J. says under her breath, exasperated at not getting another shake, "This lady has an answer for everything."

AuntMom playfully replies to T.J. when she says, "This lady is leaving for the campsite in about ten minutes, so everyone finish up. No extra milkshake, but here, both of you, take a piece or two of candy from the big bag you won at school, Michael. I brought it along for you."

T.J. replies, "Ooh, the candy, I forgot about the candy, Billy Ocean, classics. Get Out of My Dreams, Get into My Car." As she rattles off another song title. Aunt Mom cuts her off with a short, "Eat!"

Michael and 0-80 chomp away for another few minutes when AuntMom looks down at the time on her phone and says, "Everyone, quick bathroom break," as she looks at the slow moving 0-80, "and then straight to the car. We will be there in just a few more hours, and the traffic will get heavy if we don't get moving."

As the whole family wanders back to the car, Michael asks to get into the bags in the back of the small SUV that has been the family's main form of transportation for the last eight years. AuntMom lets Michael in as she opens the back liftgate. He begins to rummage through his bag, taking out a slender map, then one more map just like it. Then he takes out a fat map that has two rubber bands around it holding it together. Next, he goes in to grab a laminated map, and just then, 0-80 starts looking over Michael's shoulder and drawing attention to the proceedings.

Michael's mom says, "Just one, just pick one more map.

Have it be a little one. When you unfold those big ones in the backseat, I can't see behind me when I'm driving." 0-80 cuts in and says, "I have one you can look at. It is an old one and a special one." He tells this directly to Michael as his eyes light up and his face for the first time in many days turns from "old man" to the young and energetic twenty-nine year old that he should have been.

0-80 has the map in an envelope and whispers, "I was going to give it to you at the campsite." 0-80 directs Michael to reach into a bag in the front seat that has some of 0-80's medication in it and one singular map that has the dimensions of a magazine and is folded only one time, in half. It has been placed inside a plastic sleeve, just like the one Michael uses to cover a couple of the nicer comic books he has in his collection. 0-80 tells Michael to just look at it in the plastic while in the car and keep a good eye on it. He says, "I will tell you a wonderful story about that map when we get to the campsite. When we took pictures of that map in the old map room at the library, this map instantly came to my old senile memory."

Chapter 14

M ichael takes the map and glances at it. He imagines laying back on the hammock in 0-80's garage apartment staring at the maps on the ceiling and walls, looking at the city names, the rivers and the mountain ranges as 0-80 gives details to each place through his stories of his travels during his military service. Just about every time, he ends his stories with almost getting his backside blown to pieces. Michael doesn't think much of the fighting, just the places. He sees himself flying high above each place with a bird's eye view, or a map view of above, far removed from any fighting that might be occurring below, just soaring up and above looking down on the beautiful landscapes as he takes flight. The boy who could fly.

Michael awakens from his hazy daydream as the map that 0-80 gave him lays on his lap. The sun shines through the car window and warms his face. Michael glances down and notices the map now has a set of curious words written on it. Michael is a bit confused. He turns to T.J. to see if she may be of any help in making out some of the letters. But she is surprisingly not listening to music and has fallen asleep with her face half up against a window and half smashed into a small red blanket. She doesn't even have her earbuds in, but it still looks like occasionally she mouths a few words to a song as she sleeps.

Michael glances at the map again. The closer he looks, he can see streams and meadows and canyons and different sets of dense trees. It does look almost identical to one 0-80 and he had observed at the library, but in the lower left-hand corner are a curious string of words that wouldn't be found on any other map but this one.

This is a curious string of words Michael can not make out. He is squinting his eyes and pulling the map closer to his face to try to make out the words, and his focus is taken away from the map, from the hills, streams and mountains on the map as he glances out the window and sees the real mountain it represents in the far-off distance. He is so amazed, without noticing his own hands moving, he slips part of the map out of the plastic covering to slightly bend the map over and hold it up to the window. He is attempting to get the actual mountain to match the mountain from the background that he is looking at. As he lines the mountain and the map up against the side window, the bright sunlight makes the light words he faintly noticed before become even more visible. He takes the map out of the protective covering. He can see the curious string of letters revealing themselves around the outside border of the map. It is a numbered list, starting in the lower left-hand corner that reads:

1. on is

2. on am

3.

4. Cove

5. X

6. I

As Michael is making out the strange set of words and beginning to consider what each one means as more letters appear, 0-80 reaches around from the front seat and takes the map back from Michael. He says, "I was meaning to give that to you at the campsite. I got carried away with that sneak preview, and you saw a few words now did you? Those keen young eyes of yours, I should have known. I will show it to you and explain a few tricks to the map when we get a little time alone at the campsite."

The twist in the road and sudden steep climb startle T.J., and she wakes up. She doesn't groggily awaken, but pops her eyes open as wide as large hoop earrings. In one motion, she presses play on her music player, and T.J. is moving her head back and forth, mouthing words to a song in mere seconds.

Michael gives her a glance like she is moving a little too fast for any human to possibly move just one second after waking up. She asks AuntMom if she can roll her window down, and as she does, Michael now feels real excitement for the first time in some months as the crisp, bright, and expansive outdoor light and air have Michael thinking of flying around the places the mysterious map has shown him.

After one more stop and much aggravation, 0-80 claims

he is ready to take over the driving for the last part of the trip if it weren't for all of the upgrades in the newer cars these days, cars speeding around him in the passenger seat. He decides to stay right where he is and remind AuntMom to remain at a safe highway posted speed. The final drive toward the mountain area is on a portal road that takes the family through a bright section of a winding ride that is made brighter by the sun shining off of the sandstone and light tan rock.

The drive is majestic, continually curving around on a smooth roadway, permanently refreshing the soul as each mountain seems clearer and bigger than the next. T.J. pokes Michael in the arm and points as they both look at plenty of mountain tops– a combination of green grassy areas, and different types of rock running along various canyons. There is one high mountain with snow gleaming from its peaks.

Michael looks out the back window as his mother says they are only about twenty minutes away from the cabins and campsite. He keeps looking at the high snow filled peak far away. Nearer to him are a series of three hot air balloons that come into his view as they rise above a steep mountain face. Michael thinks to himself how wonderful and far away the balloons look, floating and flying through the air. He dreams of himself up above the hot air balloons and how it would be to look down on them from just above the middle of the three balloons. The balloons unleash a breath of fire and rise up even further in a rather loose formation. But for Michael, flying is really more than a dream. He truly feels he can fly, and he has the research to back up his belief.

Michael knows about the inverted waterfall in Chile, magnetic hill in India, and the Helium Fields in Texas. People who have flown throughout history are always on his mind. The most obvious one is Dr. Helium Skin as he is known. He did float in the air and ended up with quite a rash and talks like a squeaky mouse now. But over a number of days due to his helium experimentation, he lifted off the ground more than once. Then there was the girl caught up in a tornado who was set down without a scratch, but very dizzy, two counties over.

Now, Michael's research isn't complete, but he knows he can fly and he is serious about it. Peering back out of the car window, Michael sees the balloons drift farther away to the other side of the peak just as the car comes to the base of the steep uphill winding road that takes them to the campsite. They are traveling through a tunnel-like opening, with huge Sequoia trees that somehow are even larger and more grand than the mountains in some places. The trees part and lead to a magnificent scene. An arched rock carving spreads high above the valley floor and other round and angular mountain tops spring up in the distance. Michael's mouth opens in the back seat behind his mother. But like a ventriloquist, the sound of, "Whoa!" comes from T.J., who is sitting in the seat next to him. 0-80 turns around in the passenger seat to see Michael's mouth open, and the sound from T.J. gains an even lengthier smile than the brief one they saw earlier.

Chapter 15

The campsite is actually a large meadow that appears surrounded by the big trees and rock formations of the area. There is a small parking lot where the Jefferson family rolls their tired car to a grateful crawl and then park. T.J. is about to pop the door open right as the vehicle comes to a stop when AuntMom says, "Don't jump out into the parking lot. There are a lot of cars and campers rolling around here."

T.J. waits patiently for 0-80 to lift his aged bones out of the front seat and look both ways before he opens the door for T.J. He touches her hand as he says, "You can go over there and stretch out your voice," as he points to open pieces of grass right off the side of the parking lot. T.J. is there in a second, spinning around with her arms held out wide and loosely singing some song that seems to be titled, "You spin me round (like a record)" as 0-80 thinks to himself, in this camp of pre-teens, she may be the only one who knows what a record is.

The first of the three lead guides come to greet Aunt-

Mom, 0-80, and Michael. AuntMom calls T.J. over from her spinning top dance moves to be a part of the greeting party. The camp team of three leaders and some college assistants are scattering around talking to the young campers and their families. The camp leader that is speaking to them directly has on a large oversized floppy hat that is all green. Michael turns to T.J. and reminds her that the instructions said to bring a sun hat for all campers, but Michael says, "This guy is wearing a moon hat because if his big head gets between the earth and the sun, there is going to be an eclipse."

T.J. replies with a loud blender laugh. The hat covers the leader's large head and also has a tan drawstring attached to it that isn't pulled tight. It hangs down by the man's short but poorly trimmed beard. The second guide leader comes over and introduces himself as well. He has on a hat that can only be described as stylish and fashion-able. It is light colored. Some might call it a Panama hat, but this time T.J. is ready to provide the commentary for Michael's amusement when she calls it, "A hat for someone who is ready to deal cards." Michael smiles broadly at his younger cousin, and she looks proud of her own wit.

The most credible hat is worn by one of the college counselors, not the three camp counselors. This young man has on a more sensible hat that they both agree looks like an Indiana Jones hat. Michael wishes he had one like it himself. T.J. has bought a baseball cap that she often wears but didn't have it on. Michael has "borrowed" a hat from 0-80 that is solid in color, and Michael's mother calls it a bucket hat. She said it is okay to borrow the hat, but he shouldn't tell 0-80 he borrowed it until he gets back. 0-80 insists on calling it a "boonie" hat whenever he sees anyone wearing a hat like it.

The third guide leader comes over as the other two leaders move on to speak with different families and their campers. She wears a hat that is interesting to say the least. It really isn't a hat. It is an oversized sun visor, and she has two buns of half dark and half bleached hair sticking out from the top of her head that almost looks like she is wearing one of those mouse ear hats or even looks a bit like Minnie Mouse herself. The visor is tinted an orange-red. Michael and T.J. look at each other, amused and stunned. The visor is so odd that they both seem to struggle with coming up with a funny line for this one.

When T.J. finally says an unfunny line, "Shady Minnie Mouse," Michael takes a shot and replies, "Princess Leia welding school," as the visor has a strange hinge on it and can actually bend down to cover her face as she adjusts it to block out even more of the sun. Neither seem very impressed with their joke efforts, so they turn from the guide leaders speaking to AuntMom and 0-80. They agree that a person wearing a visor so enormous and yet functional deserves respect. So they both agree to simply call her Miss Visor until a better name comes to them. The two move away from the group leaders and meet a few college assistants as they go to look at the campgrounds together.

The campgrounds are widely varied, with the big open meadow extending for a medium length distance, and then suddenly the thickest trees and forest you may ever find. Some trails that lead all the way up to what looks like the sky and other trails that go forty feet and then stop at a set of wildflowers. All of these types of areas appear on the map 0-80 showed Michael on the car ride here.

"Plenty of places to fly around here," Michael says happily as he glances at all of the high treetops around the meadow. T.J. is equally happy. She thinks she can bop around and listen to music and sing to the birds for all two weeks of the camp. Michael and T.J. and AuntMom get excited about the time the cousins will spend here as they sit back and listen to the rules of the camp.

The camp rules are no problem at all. Michael and T.J. are very comfortable with the rules until they get to the 4th and 5th rules that are stated by the big-headed man in the even bigger hat. Michael and T.J. begin to call him The Big H for the guy with the Big head and Bigger hat. The Big H begins with the rules and others hold up signs with the rules on them.

Rule number 1 is very simple.

#1 Listen to the guides.

This isn't too much of a problem for Michael and T.J. They are both good listeners. Although in T.J.'S case, when she is reminded to listen to the guides by AuntMom, she replies, "I am a good listener. I just happen to be a good forgetter also– sometimes."

Rule 2 is as simple as Rule 1.

#2 Drink water and stay hydrated.

All agree that is a good enough idea. T.J. adds under her breath, "We might as well eat too if we are going to drink."

Rule 3, Michael and T.J. have already talked about. They were having no problem with the rules at all.

#3 Protect yourself from the sun.

That is what the mandatory hats are for. There is no problem there. T.J. has her favorite ball cap, and she put it on just a few minutes earlier. She likes to store one of her back up music players up in her hat as well, so this is a good rule for her to follow.

Rule 4 is where the problem came in.

#4 If you see bears, walk away. Don't run.

The guide with the cool panama hat took over the rules at this point. Michael and T.J. call him Little H. His head and hat are both far smaller than The Big H.

Little H carefully mentions bears are in the outdoors and how to avoid them. To pack and seal their food and— most of the kids stop listening at the point when Little H says, "If you see bears...," and a couple children audibly say, "I'm out!" or "See you later." "See you when bear season is over." As a few children actually begin to pack their own belongings, one child has already sprinted across the parking lot and is putting himself in a car seat to be driven home.

The parents who are looking forward to some "kid-free" time range from settling their concerned children back down, to getting in their faces and saying, "Well, you shouldn't have been so excited to sign up if you weren't willing to avoid a couple of bears here and there—it is the woods, by the way."

Another mother directs her child, "I told you to read the intake paperwork; I put it on the bed two nights ago. You said you read it." Her child responds, "I skimmed it! I skimmed it! You could have highlighted The BEARS part!" The mother replies, "Next time, it will be a book report on the pamphlets I give you to read. Until then, it looks like you have to deal with some nice bears." Michael is a bit wide-eyed himself thinking about the bears they may encounter, and says to himself assuredly, "Well bears can't fly, so if it comes down to it, I will have to take flight."

T.J. is fine with the bears rule. Then comes rule 5.

#5 Campers check in all electronic devices

This is where T.J. begins to lose it. "What? No music players, how? This is just like school, but for how many consecutive days? All day! I am going to need help."

AuntMom, says, "Michael will look after you, and you'll be so busy running from bears, you won't have time for any music."

Chapter 16

A ll the while, 0-80 is off staring into the dark woods. He clearly has other things on his mind. T.J. is glad that her dad came along for the ride at least to see her off. It kind of reminds her of the times when she had both a mom and a dad, and they would go to the snowless mountains in the summer with the entire family. Just as T.J.'s mind drifts back to her dad as youthful and strong, the realization of 0-80 as an old man comes back in focus as he glances over at a few campers clinging to their smartphones. He snaps at T.J., "Back when I was a camper we had maps not Apps. That's what we had out in the wilderness. There is no need for electronic devices whatsoever out here."

One of the camp counselors says, "Don't worry, sir, we have a few days and times when the devices are given to the campers so they can call and text home, but for the most part the youngsters get to enjoy nature uninterrupted by beeps, bells, and talking gadgets."

T.J. is a little discouraged about the two weeks when the counselor says most of the time would be spent without the use of technology. T.J. is so glad she has one of her best music players hidden up under her hat at that very moment. Although as she glances at AuntMom, she is sure that she will soon be busted by her seemingly all-knowing aunt who is peering directly at her hat.

After all of the direct rules were laid out, it came time for the first outdoor lessons of the camp. The camp leaders talked about respecting the outdoors and leaving no trace. They explained how you can interact and enjoy the natural surroundings without disturbing or changing it for the wildlife and future families. They will learn many skills and the importance of how to interact and become knowledge-able about all nature has to offer. There is an emphasis on important parts of camping—maintaining shelter, water, fire, and food. 0-80 chimes in to remind himself about how important survival elements are in the wilderness and life.

At this point most of the children are either still thinking about bears or have lost focus on the very talkative camp counselors. Michael has an eye toward the treetops, thinking about flying over some of the higher green branches. T.J. is singing a song in her head while talking about her own important elements to survive the outdoors and says, "My songs, music player, food and juice," when AuntMom asks if she is listening about the important elements of nature.

The man with the big floppy green hat, The Big H, comes back to the front along with the big bun visor lady, Miss Visor, and tells the families to take all of the children's bags and gear to the cabins. They can go with the children to unpack; then everyone should come back to the meeting spot for a bonfire in forty-five minutes. The word bonfire isn't recognized by all of the children, but once translated to campfire and s'mores the children forget about the bears and are thinking about the fire and the food. As T.J. is scrambling towards the cabin she is suddenly alongside Miss Visor herself and looks up at her a little fearfully, but in T.J. fashion has to ask the question that is on her mind. She asks Miss Visor, "Why is your nice hair in the big buns like that?"

Miss Visor says in an almost frightening voice, "It keeps all the big ole bugs out of my hair out here." She is trying to give little T.J. a second scare beyond the bears. T.J.'s mind is already on her next song, and she is walking away from Miss Visor unbothered by her tone of voice. T.J. does reply, but only so loud that she can hear herself and pushes her hand through her hair from the back of her head to her cheek. "I don't really do bugs, so I might have to become a bun head, too," as she walks away laughing in a low giggly laugh to herself.

T.J. is not in a cabin with Michael, but she does get a top bunk by racing by a college counselor right outside the cabin and going straight to her cabin number. The top bunk seems to make the cabin a lot nicer than it really is. She says it is about time she gets a top floor office. All the campers also get a drawer for some of their clothes and personal items and a hook on the end of the beds for their backpacks. There are two bathrooms in the cabins at the end of each hallway, and the bathrooms have more than one shower and toilet. The parents are all comfortable with the surroundings, and T.J. and Michael coming from a home with a lot of shared spaces are fine with the cabins as well.

Once semi-unpacked, the campers head outside to a pretty big fire that has already been started in a center ring of stones with flames reaching a few feet high. Considering there has been a drought the last few seasons, the fire seems to be a bad idea. However, the camp leaders appear to have it under control and later talk about extinguishing all embers and how to put out a fire safely. "But not until we feast on some more, s'mores, get it, some more, s'mores," T.J. says aloud with s'mores in both of her tiny hands and "clinks" them together to toast herself. The friendly campers don't have time to focus on the joke. Almost all of them are too busy wondering if this small but always hungry child has an extra stomach just for sugary and sweet snacks.

It is evening and getting cooler, so the fire is a nice warm light, but it isn't truly dark yet as the campers gather around the fire with their parents. The parents can stay for one more hour if they choose to. Most do, but a few say their goodbyes as the children head to sit around the camp-fire. Michael walks over to sit next to 0-80 who is near the fire and staring deeply into the orange and red glow. T.J. and AuntMom are nearby as well. T.J. is continually asking about the s'mores and says to the camp assistants, "We might as well get some hot dogs going, too."

The camp assistants begin a long interesting tale about the area. They explain some Native American names for trails and outposts. One name is that of the tallest mountain range in the area. It is called by many names but has a Native American name, Too-man-i-goo-yah which means "very old man."

Michael gets a laugh out of it and thinks instantly about 0-80. "They named a mountain peak after you, old uncle." He smiles to himself as he takes a moment to notice that 0-80 has a bit of a spark in his eye that Michael has seen a couple of times since they started on their trip.

T.J. walks over to Michael and says, "Michael, your native American name would be "Kid who says he can fly a lot." T.J.comes alive with a sudden blender laugh that gets the attention of a couple of the campers sitting near her. Before she calms herself down, she doubles over and the music player falls out from under her baseball cap that she is still wearing. She puts her hand softly on her head with a startled look on her face as AuntMom looks over at her. T.J. thinks she has been found out, but Auntmom shows some parental discretion and doesn't say anything as she slowly turns her attention back to the camp assistants who are halfway through their tale about the ancient lands.

The three camp leaders are standing up front now, right exactly in front of the fire. The glow from behind them gives a bit of a scary look to all three as they stand tall and look like a group of bandits. They are not listening to the camp assistants describe the area history as the flames lick up behind and around them and the night darkens.

The clear leader is in the green oversized floppy hat. The Big H. He has a grin on his face but looks mean at the same time. The second man still has on the smaller stylish

Panama hat, even though the sun is gone from the sky. The third lead guide is Miss Visor. She never smiles, even when she shows her teeth. She has the ability to make her voice have a very pleasant tone or a very rough one like she used on T.J. earlier. She has just taken off her visor, and it is clearly hanging down around her belt as she keeps a sharp eye on the children to make sure no one wanders from the center circle without an adult. These three leaders stand near the flames like a set of generals discussing a major plan. The Big H has returned to this exact area to finish what he started last year.

He actually started this journey three years ago. The first year of the latest series of drought years that have hikers and campers coming across items on riverbeds and low-lying streams that were exposed because of the lack of water. Usually the items found are old rusty parts of wheelbarrows or small handles from old tools, burlap bags, antique whiskey bottles and tattered remains of denim.

Last year, The Big H came on as the lead camp counselor. He also understands the area as a longtime hiker and scavenger. After years of speaking with others in the area, he continues to hear the old story about a famous wild trapper who left gold in the area. Wildman Trapper put the gold deep under the rocky bottom of a deep stream. The Big H reminds his crew of their mission. "The legend says Wildman Trapper created a way to divert the water from a deep and powerful stream just long enough to get his gold in the ground. I know there is truth in the stories and rumors. The major drought of the last few years has streams drying up more and more to the point that Wildman Trapper's lost treasure is now easier and easier to get to."

In the last year, The Big H has found a couple of slivers of gold leaf that are valuable but are not Wildman Trapper's lost treasure. He is getting desperate. With heavy El Nino storms coming soon, after this summer, the drought is sure to end.

The Big H continues his motivational speech and review of the plan. "This is the last chance with the riverbeds so dry and peeled back to get out there and dig in areas that haven't been exposed for over a hundred years."

The Big H is so desperate it causes him to call in the two other "partners" to expand his ability to search. He doesn't want to split the treasure three ways, but with big storms guaranteed to come late in the season, he thinks that splitting treasure is better than no treasure at all. "This is the year to uncover it all!" he says with an extreme passion in his voice. The flames intensify his vision and plan. They are determined to find Wildman Trapper's buried gold before the rains arrive.

The Big H and his small crew know they can use the cover of the camp children to disturb any piece of nature they want to and take things out of the area. It is easy to blame "rowdy child campers" from the city who don't know how to act in nature. These three are not a team of master treasure hunters. They are low rate but very daring thieves that are ready to blame their disruptions of sacred lands on "unruly" city kids. The plan is perfect and ready to begin. The three camp leaders break off after this discussion of how well the opening part of the undertaking is going. They slowly and quietly re-mingle with the group.

Chapter 17

Some parents dropped off the students and left as soon as the orientation ended earlier on in the day. Some left at the beginning of the campfire. But the parents did have the right to stay until a bit after nightfall if they chose to. Now, even that period of time is coming to an end, and AuntMom and 0-80 will soon have to leave. They will drive a short distance down the mountain and spend the night at a small motel at the edge of the wilderness. The next morning they will get up and spend half a day by themselves alone, just brother and sister on a road trip home trying to heal together from the traumatic last year and more that has affected their family.

With the campfire going and just a few minutes left before departure 0-80 is reminded of the time of his true youth when he was sitting around fires with his fellow recruits, or in a tent, or a shelter or an outpost. 0-80 turns from the fire, looking off on the side down a dark trail. He slowly speaks and quietly announces to AuntMom, "They send you to war at the beginning of your life, but you come back and it feels like your life is already ended, or at best you are decades older." 0-80 turns to the side, speaking to no one in particular now. "All the guys and girls, we just kind of all disappeared away." He seems like an old man looking back over a lifespan of a hundred years.

AuntMom cuts him off and says, "Alright, keep all focus going forward. You told me to remind you to talk with both T.J. and Michael before we have to go. We have about ten more minutes. I'm going to go find them for you."

0-80 for a moment stands up tall and looks almost youthful and says, "No, I will find them. You sit and enjoy this. We don't make it to the outdoors like this as much as we used to." As he glances to the side of the glowing fire and a bit behind a group of campers, he sees T.J. and Michael. The two are as close as ever sharing some jokes about the sounds they hear in the wilderness and which child will be the first snack for a hungry bear.

As 0-80 walks toward them, each step he slows as the pain throughout his body is never-ending. O-80 is shuffling forward as always. He reaches both his daughter T.J. and his nephew Michael and sits down just above them on a thick tree stump. 0-80 doesn't say hello, or how is it going, or how do you like it here so far? He just sinks down further on the stump closer to Michael and begins to speak. Michael's family is five generations of military; 0-80 reminds Michael of this now, saying, "The first military member of our family was a member of a group of soldiers that patrolled the west. They surveyed more roads and trails than Lewis and Clark, and your great-great-great grandfather was a major part of it all." 0-80 continues, "From here on," he points above the campsite, "all of it was originally mapped by them."

After a brief pause, as if 0-80 is contemplating if he should continue, he does keep speaking and says, "Years after the soldiers had all retired, some of them and your great-great- great grandfather returned to the region and made a map. When he died, it was in his will that this map would always be passed down to a family member that was also in the military. That is how it has made it to me. My father gave it to me, and now, Michael, that very map, I have here." 0-80 points to his heart. He taps inside his shirt at his heart two times and then pulls out a map from an inner pocket. I am letting you borrow this map because we are in the area. I am not giving it to you. You know I need my maps!" 0-80 concludes with a typically cranky old man punctuation in his voice.

0-80 holds the map out in front of him. He again gathers himself and continues to speak to Michael, as T.J. seems to be humming a song to herself and not paying much attention to the tale. "Now, remember, their military unit protected almost all of the western areas of the United States when it was really truly the 'old west.' It includes this land full of mountains and valleys, and desert and forest, and meadows and rivers and lakes, and the grand trees that we drove through to get here. They certainly patrolled this spot we are at right now."

Michael is staring at the folded map that is still in 0-80's hand. He is amazed that it is the same map he had held earlier in the car for a short while.

O-80 was again speaking. "They mapped entire regions as part of a special cavalry unit. They created the first marked nature trail in the national park system. I have told you about them before. They were named out of respect after the admired buffalo that roamed through many of the regions they patrolled."

0-80's voice shifts back and forth from strong soldier to current weary old man, but he continues his careful words. "Listen to me, Michael. They surveyed this entire region and mapped it all when they were young, and it was pure wilderness. They surveyed and knew every inch of this place. Then, years after they had finished their work and fulfilled their service, great-great-great grandfather and some of his fellow soldiers had a reason to return to this very region. They returned and made this."

0'80 is grasping the map very firmly now with part of a softly clenched fist. "I hold it here in my hand now." He reaches out with his empty hand, his palm up toward Michael, and Michael does the same with his hand and palm. O-80 finally says, "And now I place it in yours" 0-80 puts the map squarely in Michael's hand as he states, "The greatest surveyors of land in the history of our country, the ones who could make sense of vast wilderness and outline it to become understandable lands, maps, and trails. After all the mapping and surveying they did, they came back here, and for some reason, made a final map." He places his palm on top of Michael's hand and says, "This is the last map of the Buffalo Soldiers."

Part III

M ichael sits in disbelief. Maybe it is the outdoor environment or the energy from the warm fire, or the amount of words O-80 says to him. It is more words than O-80 has spoken to him at one time in over a year, and he still continues to speak about the Buffalo Soldiers last map that is now in Michael's hand.

"It is possible they created it for old times sake or because they forgot something they wanted to add. Maybe they all returned because they wanted to come back and retrieve something someday and this was the map to show them how to get it. Maybe it was just a last charge for the old military blood that had been running through their veins for a lifetime."

O-80 is connecting more with his younger self and speaks with a bit of a stronger and deeper voice.

His animation, his voice, and his long discussion also get T.J.'s attention. She feels a bit of the father that she barely remembers before his sudden "old age," the dad who left home again and again as an unbreakable superman and always returned even tougher and wiser. Not the injury-riddled, unfocused, forgetful dad who is friendly with the parts that are still there, but horribly missing parts that seem to be gone forever.

0-80 says with a slight tear in the corner of his left eye, "I told my father and grandfather I would follow this map to its end one day, but my old age won't allow it. In my condition, I would never get there, but I want you to borrow it for now. I was reminded of it when we saw that old map in the library. It definitely corresponds exactly to the area you are going to be in this week."

The next line from 0-80 comes with a bit of a warning.

"Maybe you don't follow it this time, but scout out the area for us, and maybe I get a little younger and stronger and you get a little older and stronger, even strong enough to fly, and we go track this map together sometime." He stops to look down at T.J. who is now under his arm. "We might even need a soundtrack for our adventure," as he winks at T.J. playfully.

T.J's heartbeat picks up a bit and the tips of her smile nearly reach each of her ears as she grins.

"Keep it folded up for now, but take a look at it tomorrow or the next day, and scout out the area when you are up a bit higher up there." He points toward one of the hiking trails and mountain peaks that aren't visible this time of night. One more thing, "When you held it up to the light in the car, you found some invisible ink they used. Remember, I told you this last map was put together by the remaining members of the cavalry soldiers that they compared to the strong roaming buffalo of the old west. They were the smartest soldiers of them all back then. I am sure this map will take some real thought to follow. I came across the invisible ink not quite as accidentally as you, and I did a little research on it with maps and what could be done around the time they were charting all of the area. They must have used some type of Algae-based ink or some type of phosphorus. It becomes faintly visible in some types of light. Remember, these were the smartest soldiers in the land, and all of their years of experience and age, and craft is right here in this last map."

0-80 painfully picks up T.J. and begins to walk with her in his arms. He tells Michael to go and say goodbye to his mom. 0-80 doesn't spend much time with T.J. because he tells himself he doesn't really know what to do with such a little girl being such an old, old man. He has not been able to find a connection yet with their newly wired family. So he says the best goodbye he can and sets T.J. down with a low moan as she runs off toward Michael and AuntMom to hug her goodbye.

As the Jefferson family members say their goodbyes, T.J. walks hand in hand with AuntMom toward her car. As they get to the dirt-covered clearing that makes for an unlined parking lot, T.J. can see that AuntMom has parked their SUV sideways in comparison to how the other cars pulled into the empty spaces earlier in the day. This is the only cue T.J. needs to go into a departing verse for AuntMom from Prince.

T.J. expects AuntMom to tell her to quiet down as her little voice carries into the darkness, but she does not. She picks up T.J. and sits her on the hood of the car so AuntMom can lean into her cheek to cheek like they are both sharing one microphone on stage. She joins T.J. just in time for the chorus to Little Red Corvette. This perfect goodbye to T.J. makes her feel like she will be okay, even with an Aunt in the place of where her mom should be.

T.J.'s song list and ratings:

Little Red Corvette

- Music 5 stars
- Singer 5 stars - He screams real good!
- Mom Meaning: <u>Having fun</u> and driving around in a car with your mom- even if it is just running errands. - have fun together. - I can hear mom saying that.

Chapter 19

The last of the parents' brake lights disappear into the distance, winding back down to a more common civilization away from the camp. The Big H scribbles down a few notes from what occurred throughout the evening. He overheard parts of the conversation between Michael and 0-80 as his ears always perk up when he hears the word map and possible additional findings in these lands. He makes sure to write down every possible idea that could lead to him getting both this new loot and Wildman Trapper's lost treasure. That is exactly what he is here for, to get treasure, not to help a bunch of kids get in touch with nature. He is hoping for some good additional finds while searching for Wildman Trapper's buried treasure and this seems to be the perfect chance.

If what Michael has in his hands is real. He has access to a map to pretty much guarantee an extra prize. The Big H takes his scribbled notes and walks in steady stride as he comes up to Miss Visor and shares what he has learned. He instructs her, "We will speak later and design an approach to get more information about this map I briefly heard about."

He leaves Miss Visor by saying, "I didn't hear it all, but it sounds like it is the lost treasure of some of the old Buffalo Soldiers. Either that, or they were probably onto the Wildman Trapper's treasure, and they figured out where to look but couldn't get to it because it was in the deep waters. Bingo! We are getting paid on this one, from the Wild Trapper, the map or both!"

The Big H thinks since he is splitting treasure winnings three ways now, this is excellent news.

He and Miss Visor walk as he decides with his devious mind what to do next. Both of Miss Visor's eyebrows are now raised at the prospect of having a full and exact treasure map as she says, "Do you think that the guy they call 0-80 is using the kids for cover the same way we are? To get to a treasure?"

The Big H is still slowly pacing with his mind on the treasures. He stops to say, "Let's just follow the kids for a day or two, keep a close eye on them. What we can do is monitor the letters they write home. We can look for any more information about the map and what this 0-80 guy plans on doing."

During the camp, all campers are required to write letters home every Tuesday, Wednesday, and Thursday to earn some electronics time during the week. They are instructed to arrive with self-addressed stamped postcards or envelopes to make sure they are ready to send letters, not emails or texts, back to their parents. The campers have designated times with the college counselors to help them write their letters to gain an hour of electronics time three days of the week during camp. The weekend has some "wildcard" time where the campers are allowed to do what they want, but even then, electronics are limited.

When it comes time to write home, Michael decides to write to both 0-80 and AuntMom. They will both know that everything is going well during the first week of camp. T.J. says she will write to AuntMom for the first two times of the week and try to write to 0-80 for her Thursday letter. T.J.'s letters give a brief idea about how camp is going the first week, but it is only a very brief idea.

T

Dear Aunt Mom,

They told me to write you 'a' letter to gain technology time, so I wrote the letter {T} above for my name.

They told me that I wasn't funny and to stop laughing. I still told them to give me my technology time (please). They didn't, so I am writing some more to use electronics and because I love my Aunt Mom...o.k. here is some more - they are still looking at me very serious face while i write...

I'm starving here, the Bears ate all the Food— send Ice Cream and MP+MMC (that's mashed potatoes and mashed macaroni and cheese- in case you forgot how we like it)!

Don't worry the Bears haven't eaten any of the kids, but there is still time.   Bye- T.J.

Letter #2 written on Wednesday

Dear AuntMom, (writing you for the same reason as letter #1)

Today we rode horses and the horse in front of me took a big old dump- Nasty.

Horses don't live here. they brought some into camp for us to ride. Do bears eat horses?

Oh yea, camp smells bad, even before the horses came and dumped all over the place. (but good news- some of the flowers smell good!)

Letter #3 written on Thursday

Dear Dad,

I don't see Michael as much here. He can do some big kid things they don't let me do here. I wish mom was still here, but glad you are still here. Come with AuntMom next week 2 pick me up.

I learned some new songs that we sang around the campfire that maybe mom didn't even know— or she forgot from when she was a little girl.

The camp songs are pretty good even though these kids sing like a bunch of amateurs. They are funny songs. I will sing them to you in the car if you tell AuntMom to let me sing in the car when I see you. Hope your head is better.

Michael's letters are a bit more informative than T.J.'s. Since it is rare that Michael ever actually mails anything through a real mailbox, he tries to write more formal letters to his family. This helps AuntMom and 0-80 better understand the actual first week experience of camp.

Dear Mom and Uncle Tony,

Hi O-80. Love you Mom. Camp is what you would think it is, we are doing all the campy things already. We have gone fishing, hiking, played Capture the Flag, skipping rocks- I'm pretty good- we have seen a lot of animals, looked at the stars-really cool!

I have had a couple of blast-offs into the sky as I have taken flight. Not even a twisted ankle when landing, so no worries there.

T.J. has been surprisingly calm, although still pretty hyper overall. Everybody has allergies, but mine aren't too bad.

Now onto the important stuff.

O-80, you were right. The map is awesome. I have seen some letters coming through very lightly on the border of the map. Here is what I have seen so far:

1. Ron Willis

2. Son Gilliam

Do you know a Ron Willis or his son Gilliam? Did our OG grandfather know them? Do you remember any stories about them?

I am going to use my phone when we have electronics time to see what I can find out. There is more writing on the map, and I am using your instructions to get them to show up. We don't have hardly any free time when it is daylight, so I can't follow all of the instructions about leaving it out in the sun, so all the letters aren't coming through yet.

We are really busy with activities during the day, but I am going to keep investigating and keep you informed about the last map, bye.

Michael- The Boy Who Says He Can Fly A Lot.

Michael's Letter #2 written on Wednesday

O-80,

I have seen a few more things already, and an adventure is definitely in order. I have found some true markers and outposts from the map <u>that are out here!</u> I have figured what I can see of the letters, but still don't know what everything means, and some letters aren't coming through. What should I do? Sunday after one week at camp, we get a free day. I will scout out a few things with T.J. and report back in my first letter next week. —Oh, here are two more numbers from the map, and letters just how they are on the last map, hopefully it makes sense to you. I still can't see number 5 and 6, Number 5 looks like it is going to be X marks the spot!

1. Ron Willis

2. Son Gilliam

3. Eat Berries

4. Cover Beehive

5. X

6.

Michael's Letter #3 written on Wednesday

Dear 0-80,

As you know, they are forcing us to write this to get electronics time. We don't get much electronics time, and I need to look stuff up on my phone so I can't spend too much time writing. Bye.

I was planning on writing more formal letters, but 0-80, I am on to something. THE LAST MAP IS REAL!

Saturday is care package day and instead of letters going out to home, campers are allowed to open all of the letters and packages that are sent to them during the week. A letter and a package comes for Michael and T.J. from 0-80 and AuntMom. 0-80 says to Michael in the letter, that he has copies of what is written on the last map from when he first investigated how the map works. He suggests just to scout out the area and find more landmarks that aren't on other maps and to be careful. 0-80 talks about how T.J.'s last letter has given him a good push to keep his recovery going. He informs Michael and T.J. "I am getting younger every day. You have a good Mom, and we have had a good week."

The letter indicates that 0-80 has even agreed to start going to his physical and other therapies again. "I can't wait to see you and T.J. when you return. I took some candy that was "stored" away by your mom and put it in the package for you and T.J. Still don't go flying around but take off and explore while you are out there," is how he ends his portion of the letter to Michael and T.J.

The final paragraph of his letter is addressed directly to Michael only, and it tells him, "Your young Uncle Tony plans on coming back out there with you soon, maybe even later this summer." The p.s. in the letter gives Michael almost all he needs to have every detail from the last map when 0-80 writes:

Here are all sets of letters on the map. There is one last one that tells me you should be really careful and just scout it out. There are 6 total. You did great to get the first 4. I will give you number 5 and 6 since it is coming up on your last week of camp, but number 6 seems like it is a bit ominous—if you know what that word means—it means possibly dangerous.

You should wait for me when I am around and get to be a bit younger to complete all of the map for real. Your mom probably wouldn't want me to give you the last one, to be honest, but I trust you. You have in your hands the mapped ways of your great-great-great grandfather and information of the last map. See number 5 below, sorry to inform you, it is not X marks the spot:

1. Ron Willis
2. Son Gilliam
3. Eat Berries
4. Cover Beehive
5. X Ray Late Day
6. I + Would + Not = Enter

Michael is stunned as he reads all six items. He has every component and word the map has to offer. He is excited to put the map and his notes to work with the free day on Sunday coming up tomorrow.

Chapter 20

The diabolical camp leader that Michael and T.J. continue to call The Big H takes notes during the week as well. His big hat hangs low over his eyes as he tries to hide his villainous nature. He continues his calculating day by day and approaches his other partners with a plan for Sunday as well. He tells them about Michael's notes and mail throughout the week.

"Checking them to make sure he wrote enough to gain electronics time," is what he says.

The Big H spends the week planning for an adventure with his two equally dishonest partners, Miss Visor and Little H. By reading 0-80's letter to Michael, The Big H has the same six items from the list that Michael does.

He uses the cover story that they inspect children's belongings to make sure they don't have any open food that will attract bears. The Big H even takes a Twinkie and two homemade chocolate chip cookies from a care package and later sneaks off to eat them in front of Miss Visor saying, "Looks like I got to them just in time to keep the bears away." He makes his comment while deviously laughing with a mouth full of stolen snack food.

The Big H writes down so much of the map that he has the first part of the map memorized just by being nosey and looking at the map when spying on Michael daily. The map has many of the peaks, plateaus, lakes, valleys, forest, canyons, and natural landmarks of the area that he has seen on other maps. But it also has more than a few areas that are unknown and never seen on any other maps of the area. There are different trails on the map to follow, but no single trail to lead them directly to a treasure. He tells his partners, "Even with the map in hand, to complete it and get the reward will take some navigation for sure."

"It can be pretty rough and remote up here. A wrong trail or misstep could have you walking around for days in a forest, cavern, canyon, or worse," Miss Visor says as she slaps at a little bug that lands near her knee.

The Big H finishes the conversation saying, "I know. We need to get the actual map in his hands to reveal all of its secrets, but I also know enough about the area to keep us safe. Don't worry."

The Big H spends some time during the week walking the first part of the trail, thinking about the map. He checks outposts and unique map trails to see if they really match what is up in this area. So far, he confirms that the map matches the exact part of the land they are near.

The Big H debates with his crew about taking the map and just abandoning the campers for a day or two and going to see what they can find. He discusses the problem with Little H and Miss Visor. They all believe Michael has a better chance of figuring out the items than they do. Also,

Michael never lets the last map out of his possession the entire time at camp. He even puts it in a double plastic bag and hides it in an extra towel he takes with him into the shower stalls. The map is always in his eyesight.

The Big H and his team continue the plan that they will grab the map when Michael is on one of the trails. "Once he is in that deep wilderness, whatever we have to do to get the map and get the answers for the number 1 through 6 on the map will have no witnesses."

The Big H makes sure his partners understand. He looks at Little H to make sure he is paying attention. "You are to follow Michael if he ever scouts out the area further like his uncle told him to in his letter. See what he can solve. This kid knows something we don't."

Miss Visor continues to discuss strategy and says, "If we have to get violent with the young ones, I can handle that. We can go take the map right now, get the treasure, and even return the map to Michael or his uncle later. We can tell him that nothing was found, but we had to take it because Michael was wandering off too far because of it. Let him and his uncle come back later in the year and go rumbling around for a treasure that is no longer there!"

"I have seen the map more than anyone," The Big H says. "It has a lot of different paths and trails and areas. Having the map without having the knowledge will do us no good, unless you are prepared to go on a forty day hike." He looks at Miss Visor and her perfectly kept hair and Little H and his perfectly out of shape stomach. He finishes the meeting with, "Just follow my instructions and report everything you see or hear back to me."

For now The Big H keeps on trying to figure out what

all of the items he has written down mean. He looks at the numbers 1, 2, 3, 4, 5, 6.

1. Ron Willis
2. Son Gilliam
3. Eat Berries
4. Cover Beehive
5. X Ray Late Day
6. I + Would + Not = Enter

To the Big H, it seems cruel to him that he has spent the last three years looking for Wildman Trapper's lost treasure without much of a payment in return. This is his big chance for a double payment. The Big H is still confused about the lettering and how it appears and disappears. Michael seems to have it all figured out as more letters appear throughout the week. The Big H has to admit the kid is pretty sharp.

Chapter 21

Sunday is a free day at camp. T.J. looks forward to spending time with Michael. Even though the last week has been fun for T.J. because it has been different, she has not spent this much time apart from Michael in the last year. She especially misses him at night when they would talk to each other through the very thin plywood wall that separates their rooms. Here at camp the girls and guys sleep in separate cabins, so Michael is not there to speak quietly to her as she falls asleep, and he is not the first comforting voice that she hears in the morning.

You would think with all of the songs in her head, T.J. could control her thoughts at night by playing a song or two in her mind while she falls asleep. She goes over her song list ratings journal every night. As much as she likes the songs, unfortunately, at night it is a challenge for her to keep her thoughts totally upbeat. That is where Michael always comes in, knowing he is so close as she closes her eyes and drifts off to sleep.

It has been this way since the first night T.J. came to live with them in their house. All the way back to that first night when he heard her quietly crying and asking why she couldn't stay in the garage with her dad. They weren't even trying to keep the truth from her, but eventually Michael just read her the entire letter and hospital information that AuntMom read to him when she told him 0-80 would be a permanent part of the family, and they would be fixing up the garage for her brother "Uncle Tony" to live in. T.J. didn't get all of it, but Michael made it clear she understood.

Multiple deployments means you never give up. Purple Heart means you are tough. Honorable Discharge means he did really good all the way to the end. He quickly skipped over parts she wouldn't get like post traumatic syndrome, cerebrum, blunt trauma, embedded shrapnel, temporal nerves. Michael did try to sum it all up by saying as kindly as he could, just quickly summarizing a hard hit on the head means you probably, maybe, will never really remember most things the same ever again and could shuffle around like an old man for some time before you start to get better.

Whenever Michael brings any of these items up to his mother, it is always the same response, "With medical advances" AuntMom always says, and "with consistent rehabilitation" she always adds. Michael thinks as the family ultimately does. It is better for everyone and T.J. to not think of Tony as the strong young dad who would throw the football a mile for Michael or pick up his wife and daughter at the same time and spin them around, making T.J. hit two or three of her many laughs with each twirl.

It is better to cope by just having him be 0-80—a bit absent-minded and shuffling, snapping a response from time to time, but still a good part of the family. A person who enjoys his maps and his naps and is almost always on time for dinner when his nephew Michael or his sister-caretaker AuntMom tell him it is time to eat.

As soon as the counselors allow the campers to go out of their cabins, Michael takes a giant leap off of his cabin's front porch. He bounds straight up in the air and then comes down softly. He heads straight to T.J. She skips and floats on air a bit herself as she races toward her cousin, knowing they have a full day together.

For breakfast and lunch, Michael and T.J. eat in the dining cabin at different times because they are in different age groups. They have seen a bit of each other this week in the evening because dinnertime has all campers eat together. During "free day" breakfast is all together. Lunch is a sack lunch they can have whenever they want to. Dinner is around a big campfire just like they had on the first night. This time it will include hot dogs!

"Teeeee.Jaaaaaaaay, it is you and me all daaaaaaaay," Michael yells as they approach each other.

T.J. giggles as she likes the excitement in her cousin's voice as he calls her name, and she likes the intentional rhyme of Michael's sentence.

"T.Jaaay it is you and me all daaaay," she repeats. "We should write that one down. I like the sound of that. I could sing that line a lot."

Michael goes directly into his plan of action for the day and says, "Today will be a grand adventure that was set up by the last map of our great-great-great grandfather!"

Despite Michael's big set up, T.J. responds, "I thought we would maybe just go skip some rocks over by the big lake while I listen to music and you fly around. But whatever, I am with you today."

She pauses and slyly pulls a music player from inside of her hair as she lifts her hat, "Well, I am with you and my music player."

Michael takes a hard look at her hat and comments, "I thought no music players are a part of this trip for you. AuntMom says you will have severely damaged eardrums by the time you are a teenager."

T.J. says, "I haven't even used it that much this week. I can only charge it an hour or so during electronics time, and that day it was really cloudy, I had to leave it hidden under my pillow because I forgot my hat to sneak it outside with."

The music players remain important to T.J. In her mind every song she listens to she can still hear her mother's voice blend with the vocals of the artist. "Every time I sing a song, it's me and my mom." T.J. always joined in for the chorus when they sang together. No matter how hard she tried, she wasn't able to memorize all of the lyrics as well as her mom. Now she has memorized almost every song from every playlist her mother had but doesn't have a mom to sing along with.

What she does have is Michael and a recovering spirit that they have both seen spread to 0-80 from time to time. Maybe there is something to "medical advances" and "rehabilitation" and most importantly a hopeful spirit.

As the two cousins reunite and look over their supplies for the day. They see a backpack full of granola bars and some camping items, including a compass, two flashlights and two "pocketknives." They have a separate backpack that the college counselors like to call a camelback. It is just for holding water.

Another group reunites as well. All three of the villains in their signature hats and visor are watching over the campers as they begin to talk about their free day activities. Different hiking trails are available to the campers, depending on your age group and depending on the college counselor who is leading your hike. The archery area is open for two hours in the morning. There is an arts and crafts table set up, and a game of kickball that will be starting soon along with other organized free day activities.

This leads T.J. to say, "Leave it to AuntMom to send us to a place where even the free day is completely organized!"

Michael says, "Don't worry, I told you. I have an organized plan of our own, and it is based on the organization of this." He shows the map inside his light vest and slightly lifts it out of his pocket. This little glimpse of the map is exactly what The Big H is looking for. His eyes turn into sharp little beads as he stares down exactly where Michael replaces the map. When he sees it, he turns to his two other thieves who are about fifteen feet away and makes a sharp noise to get their attention and says, "Pssst-hey, hey! This is our time guys. He is doing what he talked about in his letter and going out with the map. Keep all attention on the kid who thinks he can fly."

As they all start to turn their gaze to Michael and T.J., The Big H suddenly lifts his head toward the sky. A fairly clear morning has now begun to display a few thick clouds miles off to the west.

The Big H says gruffly, "If it starts to rain, or even looks anymore like rain, we will have to make a move on the boy."

"Yes, for sure," Miss Visor replies. "It is hard enough to find Wildman Trapper's treasure when it is dry. If the rains come early and the streams and rivers return to normal levels, it will be nearly impossible. Let's not be afraid to do whatever we have to get the map and Wildman Trapper's prize."

The Big H cuts in and continues the harsh tones. "They are saying this year the drought will end. Rains are coming. We have to get this done now, this week, no later!"

Miss Visor jumps in and adds a final sudden statement, "The kids are, let's say, removable. There are a lot of trails they can 'accidentally' fall off and over the side of high cliffs."

While making this declaration, The Big H moves his attention to a small lockbox he pulls out of his knapsack. He turns his back to the camp but is still in clear view of Little H and Miss Visor. He looks both of them in the eye when he opens the lock box to grab not gold, but a more dangerous prize. Miss Visor looks excited and leans in. Little H takes a step back when he sees what appears from the lock box. The Big H takes out a small handgun and shoves it down inside the front of his outdoor jumpsuit and quickly zips the front of it back up.

Chapter 22

With a free day in full motion, Michael and T.J. do a few general activities and wander from group to group as the other students do the same. Soon a couple of different college counselors are to go off with groups into the woods to look for certain types of flowers and birds. Michael and T.J. know the college counselors do not have anywhere near the instinctive superpowers that AuntMom has.

It has been fairly easy to get away with random acts of trickery, like hidden music players and staying up past curfew during the week. Michael and T.J. have no trouble getting the Group A counselor to believe they are going hiking with Group B. At the same time they get the Group B counselor to think they are going hiking with Group A. This allows them to slip off to a separate trail entirely. A trail that is only on the last map. The trail has a very steep incline to climb at the beginning. It quickly gets them to a back part of the wilderness that is laid out on the last map.

As soon as they reach the top of the steep incline which

surprisingly takes over an hour, very little words are heard between the two cousins, except T.J. singing under her breath. Michael's excitement remains, even though he realizes this is going to be more than an adventure down to the library with 0-80 to look at old maps. Michael now stood in the place the maps were created.

Michael can't help but hear the voice of 0-80 in his head,

"Got my backside shot off running through places like that!"

Now, after this hour plus of steep climb, Michael is right in the middle of one of those places. They reach the top of the steep incline after a week of clues, and ideas, and thoughts, and hopes. They find it easier to navigate now that they are on flat ground and the area has some green moss-covered rocks but not an abundance of trees.

Michael pulls out the last map and unfolds it completely as it arrives in full glory. The map seems to match the area almost in an eerie fashion, considering it had to have been made sixty, seventy, or even eighty years ago. Michael feels connected to the Buffalo Soldiers of old as he reviews many different forest areas on the map. He looks at canyons that are outlined—rocky areas, streams, waterfalls, lakes, geysers and much more. Right in front of them is an immediate arch of trees that leads to a clear but narrow forest path. It does not look untraveled, but about fifty feet down the path it looks to become even more narrow. It is a path that is on the last map only. Michael says, "We are in the last map territory for sure now. This won't be the only set of trees we hit today." He and T.J. walk on the path with a bounce in their step.

Unlike Michael and T.J., The Big H and his team find no surprises with the steep climb because The Big H scouts out the initial area near camp more than a few times before any children arrive. They are easily able to let Michael and T.J. move ahead without any problems keeping them in range. Now as Michael reaches the top of the steep incline and pulls out the last map, the three begin to salivate with greed. Their hands and fingers all unconsciously begin to move like they are handling money at a bank. Little H can picture having gold coins fall into his hands. He whispers, "Cha-Ching, Cha-Ching" every few seconds as he sees the money falling into his hands like he is collecting winnings from a slot machine. Little H reaches deep into his pocket like he is going to pull out a big wallet full of money. He only finds pocket lint in his palm when he pulls out his hand from his pants. The lint floats off with the wind.

Their thoughts of money make them immediately discuss closing the space between themselves and Michael and T.J. and either taking the map outright or demanding that the two serve as forced guides to read and understand every bit of the last map and lead them to the treasure.

Before they even get the chance to take any action, Michael and T.J. follow the last map trail down the narrow path and into a new forest with rows of tight trees. All three villains are slowed by the narrow path into the forest. The path even causes the shortest of the three, Little H, to duck down through many parts of the trail section.

The paths become a bit of an unknown advantage for Michael and T.J. because their smaller size makes the tight space with so many overhanging limbs easier to walk through. Even though it is only now becoming midday, some darkness comes over Michael and T.J. as the sun struggles to shine through the tops of the forest trees, and light struggles to make it all the way to the forest floor. When the sun does come through, it creates thick tunnels of light that warm up entire areas in the forest. Then instantly the forest trail goes back to being a land of cool shade with cool winds blowing leaves around their feet.

Michael and T.J. eat through their supplies with all the energy it takes to keep on hiking. The trail gets more frightening and more fun as the two cousins agree to go forward together.

T.J. says, "I thought you said this was going to be a forest trail. A forest we can find about twenty minutes away from the big park not too far from our house."

Michael says, "Those are woods. This is a forest." T.J. says, "This ain't no forest, this is a jungle." T.J. begins to call the forest a jungle. "It sounds better to say you are lost in a jungle than in the forest," was her final point.

This is definitely more consuming than any woods or forest they have ever run through, and it seems to have no end despite the map showing they should be out of the area already. Michael doesn't say it, and he doesn't even sense it, but he does think that maybe the last map isn't as real as he first thought it was?

Chapter 23

The fact Michael believes he can fly always seems to him to be the comforting grace he has to get out of what is becoming a mess of a trail. The trail is so tight now that even Michael and T.J. have to duck down and even crawl through a few tight parts of it.

"The tree limbs are like long fingers that are purposely stretching out to scratch us," T.J. says,

Michael stays upbeat, thinking about flying through the air as the wind is heard whipping around the trees with a low whooshing sound. Michael knows he can fly, but T. J., who is stuck with him, couldn't. What T.J. can do and continues to do is sing from the incredible library of songs she has in her head. This is her saving grace. T.J. is still humming along behind Michael. What she lacks in musical tone, she makes up for in the catalogue of songs in her head, mainly older tunes, her memorable delivery, and ability to hit some incredible notes from time to time. T.J. always seems to have just the right song, or the wrong song depending on your point of view, on the tip of her tongue at any moment.

T.J. doesn't look the part of a singer. She is both small and lanky which is hard to achieve. She now stands with a battered maroon baseball cap on her head with the mud and dirt from the "jungle" coming closer every moment she goes forward. She wears light denim shorts that are so long they come all the way down to her almost knee-high socks. These socks have two blue rings to match her denim shorts about a half of an inch wide toward the very top of them. T.J.'s socks slip down during the day in the forest jungle.

From time to time, T.J. pulls the blue striped socks up to repel bug bites and rough branches and leaves in the "jungle." As the day gets longer., T.J. let's out a groan, "Uggh, these socks." At one point, the socks are down more than they are up, and T.J. is too tired to do anything about them.

It isn't the clothes that or socks or the gold Converse high tops she wore that kept T.J. going. She returns to the catalogue of songs playing over and over in her head. They are seemingly lost under the canopy of deep dark jungle as Michael and T.J. are looking out through the interruptions in the big enveloping trees and roots hanging overhead at the sky.

A few simple light raindrops fall. They walk but now feel the ground under them touched by a brief, soft rain. Enough small drops of rain make it through the heavy cover overhead and run down the leaves and trees to make the ground a bit muddy and even harder to walk through. They are still on a path of some kind, but now the leaves and forest are so close, they are walking in a single file line. This makes it even more likely that Michael and T.J. will not be found anytime soon if they are indeed lost.

They march forward through rough trails and tough sawgrass. They are tired, but still in good spirits. They discuss camp so far. They turn the conversation to the college counselors and how nice they are. They are glad they came on this trip.

"AuntMom came through again," T.J. says.

"The only problem so far has been a couple of the ones in charge."

"I know, Little H for one. He's had beans on his chin everyday for like three days. Everytime after he eats. Yuck," Michael says.

"Actually, I think they were the same beans stuck to his chin from the first day! Super Yuck! Enough about him," T.J. decides.

"Well, that Miss Visor is a weird one. She looks nice when she isn't looking at you, but angry in her expressions when she is." Michael hunches over as he fights through more grass that has overgrown the trail.

T.J. says, "I know, she tries to smile and it looks crusty."

Michael adds. "It's her eyebrows. I think she paints them on. They are dark. You shouldn't paint your forehead."

T.J. is now having fun. "Yea, Miss Visor's eyebrows look like they have never lost a fight."

"What do you mean?" Michael says-

"They are strong!" T.J. loudly replies.

Michael is cracking up and then says, "Come on, T.J., I'm going to lose all my energy laughing."

T.J. is also becoming tired, but the light refreshing rain

is helping, and she is not too tired to laugh. When she finishes her joke, she still uses her remarkable laugh, like a blender chopping its way through fruits and berries while making a smoothie. This laugh serves as a decent marker for their three pursuers, who are well equipped to hike and track Michael and T.J. for days.

The rain is falling on the three villains. This does not refresh them at all. It only makes them mad. The rain drives Miss Visor into a momentary frenzy. She knows the rains are coming. Even a couple days of rain can have streams and rivers refill to the point it would be impossible to track down Wildman Trapper's treasure at the bottom of a riverbed.

Little H says what everyone's thinking. "If the only treasure we are going to get is from that map, we better go get those kids." They all are instantly more ruthless and more intent in their actions toward Michael and T.J., as the mere possibility of losing Wildman Trapper's buried treasure arrives. Little H unfolds a medium sized metal walking stick from the pack he is hiking with. This stick is also a handy weapon. He is using it to clear away branches and brush ahead of Miss Visor and The Big H who are walking behind at a very even and observant pace. The Big H declares in a calculating and menacing voice, "This changes everything!" He commands Little H and Miss Visor that "We will overtake the two young kids and finish this today if any more rain shows up."

With those words Miss Visor pulls out and unfolds her

own walking stick from her equally sized pack and moves up alongside Little H. Her stick also appears to be very usable as a weapon as well. It is similar to the metal one Little H is using, but Miss Visor's stick has a sharper side to it as well. She is slashing away at the forest at twice the rate and three times the anger as Little H as they hurry to catch up with Michael and T.J. The Big H still looks under control after these bursts of aggression. He is back calculating and thinking of how the plan will play out very soon.

The minimal rain stops. The tight trail starts to widen every few hundred feet, and Michael thinks this means they are soon going to make their way out of the forest and this tough part of the journey. He is correct. Even with Michael and T.J. heading toward exhaustion at their current pace, the two friends continue to find plenty of things to laugh at together. This is one of those times when after hours of walking, the forest trees finally open up, and Michael sees a clearing slanting down away from them. He says, "T.J., it will be good to be able to walk downhill for a while. Look ahead over there."

As the trees become further spread apart and the clearing is becoming more visible, even more important than walking downhill is the sound of moving water ahead. Michael starts to slowly run. He runs down the first part of the slope just before coming out of the trees and speeds up with the momentum from going downhill. He is moving so fast he almost bumps his head on a low-lying branch. When he looks back to see how close he came to bumping his head, he trips over a log and slides headfirst, like a major league baseball player, right up to a frog that lets out a loud "ribbit" and then jumps over his head. T.J. laughs and laughs and laughs out loud and calls ahead to Michael, "Don't worry, I waited until I saw that the frog was okay before I started laughing."

The frog jumping off into the distance leads Michael and T.J. from a tiny stream to the first mini-waterfall they come across. The waterfall is down to a light trickle due to the slight rain that can't make up for the drought-like conditions. It does provide enough water for refills and the ability to clean off some of the dirt from the trek through the forest.

Even with the flow of water not being strong, the sound of the water is continual and constant and gives the area a great sense of renewal. It shows how even a slight flow of energy in the right direction can go toward energizing life. The water falling from the sky filled in a few old grooves where it looked like nothing would ever come alive again. The find is well worth being ridiculed by a frog after sliding down a slippery hill. T.J. continues to wash some of the dirt out of her clothes. The stream and small amount of rain they encounter guarantee they should never be too long without water. It was warmer out in the open than under the trees and a bit humid after the brief rainfalls. The water was a great refresher, and the humidity would not last long as the hottest part of the day was behind them after such a long hike.

Another sprinkle of rain starts again while they are at the small waterfall. This exciting development gets another full song by T.J. as they are both happy that they survived and escaped the forest trail. They can feel the moisture and they both look up to let the refreshing rain touch their faces. T.J. opens up her mouth and sings to the sky as she splashes

Michael with water from the waterfall to a song from New Edition, Can You Stand the Rain as they dance around for a few moments of fun.

T.J.'s songlist and ratings:

Can You Stand the Rain

- Music 4 and ½ stars
- Singers: 5 stars
- Mom Meaning: Hang in there. We are in this together. - I can hear mom saying that.

Chapter 24

M ichael and T.J. combine lunch and dinner by eating most of the two boxes of granola bars and other assorted snacks they'd crammed into Michael's backpack before they left. They feel tired, dirty, and worn out, but grateful that they came across the slight waterfall and shallow stream with drinking water to quench their thirst and fill up their sixty-four ounce camel water pack. This is done first due to 0-80 reminding them that the most valuable resource in nature is water. The water pack is on Michael's back and also sometimes in the bigger backpack with only the drinking straw from the water pack sneaking out from under the bigger backpack.

Neither seems to be practicing any sort of water conservation. Not thirty minutes goes by without one or the other reaching for the long straw-like feeding tube curling from around Michael's back from the camel pack and taking long sips of water. The last map shows the area where they are with the mostly dried-up stream on it, so they walk along the stream path for a short time. One benefit of going through supplies is that the regular backpack is becoming lighter and lighter. From time to time, T.J. wants to carry the water pack but ends up carrying it for only a few minutes. Michael finds the drinking straw from the water pack curled around in front of T.J. is too tempting as a microphone and seems to inspire the likelihood of even more boisterous singing by T.J.

Michael says, "I have no intentions of getting tracked down by someone or something wild out here because of your very loud and animated version of Man in the Mirror" as she sings through the chorus of a Michael Jackson song looking at herself in the shallow but reflective stream.

Michael and T.J. both hear noises behind them throughout the day. They definitely did hear real slashing animal sounds coming from behind them at one point when walking through the forest. The sounds came from Miss Visor and Little H as they cut and beat their way through the area while following the two. Michael and T.J. agree they are probably being tracked by bears from time to time. So far, they have only seen the trees rattle and shake behind them, but have not seen any large animals, which is a very good thing. They do take stock of their travel belongings for any weapons they have. As expected, they do not have too much to fight off bears. They both have "pocketknives" that fold out. T.J.'s "pocketknife" only really has a fork and a spoon that fold out and has no real knife anyway.

T.J. angrily remarked when she received it from AuntMom and 0-80, "You might as well call it a pocket-spork. It can't be a pocketknife. See, as a pocketknife it just doesn't cut it!" T.J. starts to laugh hilariously, remembering and repeating her line to AuntMom and 0-80, and says, "I just lol'd myself," as she continues to laugh and laugh. The pocket knives are so small, a bear would only use them as a toothpick after it finishes eating them for a meal. They both stop and listen and look for bears. Luckily at first, they don't hear or see anything, so they continue with a review of their supplies.

Then T.J. says, "I see a baby bear!"

Michael says, "What? Where? I don't see anything, but if you are right, momma bear won't be not too far behind."

Michael quickly pushes T.J. up in the nearest tree and is about to fly up next to her when he turns around to check for any bears that might be reaching for him. He immediately stops all his action and says, "T.J. is that the bear?"

"Yeah, look out for his momma!" T.J. issues another quick warning.

Michael looks around and up at T.J. with no tension or fear in his body at all. Once he flashes one more look to be sure, he immediately turns to T.J. and says in a distressed and tired voice, "T.J., That is a racoon!"

T.J. is still poorly trying to climb up the tree. "No, I am pretty sure it is a baby bear. Look, it has claws, one of those soft bear noses, and fur. That is the definition of a bear.

Michael doesn't know why he tries to debate her, but he argues back and says, "Look at the fur, around the eyes. That is the unique fur mask of a racoon."

"A fur mask!" T.J. yells back, yeah, I see it now," as she starts to climb down. "But it wasn't that clear before. If a wild animal is coming for you, I check for claws first and the fur mask second."

Michael says, "So you agree it is a racoon, come on down. I will help you-"

"I'm not sure, I still think it is a lot like a bear. It could even be a bear-coon. We should be careful. It is half bear and half racoon."

Michael says, "there is no such thing, T.J."

T.J. quickly defends herself and says, "Not true. My friend in school has a labradoodle. We should call this monster a bear-coon."

Michael replies, "I will not call it a bear-coon, and I am going to talk to your teacher. They aren't teaching you what a racoon is in your class?"

T.J. is down at the base of the tree still muttering, "It's hard to tell them apart when they aren't on flash cards! I see it is like a racoon, now, but can we agree it is a racoon with bear qualities...?"

Michael says, "No."

T.J. is still talking, "I'm pretty sure we both heard it growl." Michael says nothing further to end the play argument and bring their tiring focus back to follow the small trail.

Chapter 25

The sun is already halfway down in the distant sky. A scout mission is now about to turn into a nighttime mission and a two-day affair. "We are in the biggest trouble of our lives." T.J. is right about that. Being out at night gets pretty dark. The most important part of the supply check for Michael and T.J. is to review food and water. They have some food left with some half-eaten granola bars. Michael finds a bunch of trail mix still sitting in the bottom of the backpack. He has no idea where it came from.

T.J. says, "Surprise!"

Maybe it isn't much of a surprise considering one of T.J.'s major goals for the week is to eat a bunch of trail mix while actually on a hiking trail. She often questions AuntMom when they are back home, "Hey, why do they call it trail mix? We hardly ever eat the stuff on any type of trail. Why don't they call it couch mix? Most people eat it like us, sitting here on a couch." She wants to start a campaign requiring people to call it couch mix or sitting mix unless you really have been out hiking at some point while eating part of your current bag.

Before they left in the morning T.J. overloaded three large plastic bags with trail mix. She hid it in the bottom of the bag under the off white towel when Michael wasn't looking. "To make up for all of the times I was eating 'couch mix,'" is what she tells Michael. This extra food is almost all that is left.

The darkness in the wilderness is much different than being back home. The open sky is getting dark, but overhead is filled with so many stars and a strong almost full moon that light seems to still be available as the sun finally goes down. The night is not too scary for Michael and T.J. with the glow from across the sky. Michael and T.J. reach the end of the stream. Up on the other side is more elevation surrounding a rocky path that is also on the last map.

Luckily this part of the hike is not steep and the rocky path leads up to a series of big rocks and even a few caves. The path is not very difficult to walk, but their flashlights are not military grade according to 0-80. They are only able to shine a few feet ahead of them clearly.

"Whoops," is heard more than one time from T.J. as she slips on the loose pebbles without being able to see as well at night. Then, "Oops," then "oopsie."

This convinces Michael to look for a place to stop and find shelter. They check a short cave with their flashlights in hand and the light of the stars behind them. They both make sure it is empty before agreeing it seems to be the best place for them to rest for the night.

As night sets in Michael and T.J. both initially are concerned about how it would feel to sleep outside. Being tucked away in a quiet cave looking out at the calm stars has them both feeling fine. They are okay with where they are and the peace that it brings them after a long difficult day. They are on an adventure they accept.

Michael does start to worry about T.J. and to worry about all of the speeches and lectures he will hear from AuntMom. He is beyond beginning to worry about the last map. The trail they are on seems to be real and match the map, but they haven't found anything to even begin to lead them to the words on the map. He knows they will have a hard hike back tomorrow and will never be allowed to go anywhere but to school and home for the next ten years of their lives.

Michael takes out the list, and he decides to look it over to see if they missed any of the items during the long day. They sit in the cave eating handfuls of trail mix.

1. Ron Willis
2. Son Gilliam
3. Eat Berries
4. Cover Beehive
5. X-Ray Late Day
6. I + Would + Not = Enter

He feels T.J. crawl up next to him and is about to ask her about all of these worries. He thinks she is coming closer to him because she may be getting scared as night continues. He is prepared to comfort her. Instead, T.J. flips on the flashlight. She points it at her face and starts in with Michael Jackson's Thriller. He laughs as T.J. knows exactly what she is doing, and as always, she is just happy to be anywhere with her cousin Michael with not much of a worry at all.

She says, "Fun day, long day. I guess we hike back tomorrow and then just be in trouble for the rest of our lives. If we start to think up a story now, we should have a good one by tomorrow. It may sound crazy, but listen to my idea very closely. I just need you to confirm one thing. Do you know if AuntMom believes in Bigfoot?"

Michael smiles at the effort but announces openly before T.J. continues with a wild plan, "No. AuntMom is a definite no on Bigfoot."

T.J. doesn't let that stop her planning stages. "Hmmm?" she reacts, "Sinkhole or quicksand, which one sounds more believable to you?"

Michael brings the conversation back to reality with a bit of disappointment in his voice. "Either way, no matter what happens, we tried, but we didn't really find one of these clues, did we?"

For better or for worse, after not being next to each other at night for a week, falling asleep side by side, even in a cave under the stars, felt a lot like home. They both confirm that they are not scared but keep one of the flash-lights on as a night light, just in case they need to see some wild thing charging at them. Michael and T.J. split a short blanket that T.J. pulls out of somewhere.

"It is for a picnic I planned on having, a glorious trail mix picnic while hiking on a trail." And she unfolds the blanket towards Michael so they can share. The flashlight runs out of power, and the cave goes dim as they both fall asleep almost immediately without another word between them.

Chapter 26

I t is easy for the villains to follow the muddy footprints
along the stream and waterfall and stay on Michael and
T.J. 's trail. During the long day, The Big H hasn't even
taken out his binoculars to track them. Now for the first
time, he does take the time to put his organized backpack
down and pull out the binoculars. He watches Michael and
T.J. through hidden lenses as they climb up the rocky trail
and into a cave. The other two villains lay down their backpacks also. They are very well packed. They are fully
prepared for a night, or nights in the outdoors. They are
not professionals, but The Big H has experience hiking and
camping. They know to head back a bit to make their camp
just a few hundred feet from the water.

One smart sneaky move the Big H makes is to radio
back to camp saying they noticed Michael and T.J. went
missing, and they are out searching for them. He says there
is no need to call a search party yet. The Big H tells his
most responsible college counselor. "We will likely find
them. We have seen their footprints and trail. If they are

too far away from the camp when we find them, we will spend the night out in this area and then walk back with them tomorrow." The Big H repeats, "There is no need to call a search party of any kind. We are moving beyond cell phone range. We will lose our signal, so you may not hear from us for a while, but all should be fine tomorrow." The Big H finishes his call and turns to Little H and says, "That will give us all the time we need to take care of our business with the kids and the map.

They set up their camp to have the stream as a morning source of water energy for themselves. They can use it to wash up and for hot meals. Despite their medium size packs, all three pull out and unroll small individual sleeping bags that are also like tents. Miss Visor says, "We are looking at a good meal and a good night's rest down here compared to those kids. They will be so scared and tired and sore. They will probably give us the map tomorrow morning and beg us to help them get out of here."

The Big H says, "Yes, and if not, we will take the map or move out ahead of them tomorrow morning. This rain surprised me today. There may be some more afternoon showers tomorrow. One way or the other, tomorrow, we end this."

All three get up early the next morning, and their minds are unchanged. They confirm they will do whatever they have to with Michael and T.J. to get the treasure that may be at the end of the last map trail. Miss Visor even keeps her hair in the buns all night long! She doesn't want any bugs in her hair or to waste any time. They are all ready to get up and go.

The three villains are frustrated but not tired from the

day before. If anything they are well-rested and ready to track down the two cousins. Little H goes out early to scout ahead and make sure that Michael and T.J. haven't moved out too far from the cave in front of them. He doesn't see any sign of them stirring yet, so he returns to the camp and informs The Big H. All three take the time to eat a quick meal and have a cup of coffee over the small fire they make for cooking. They utilize the morning winds to make sure any smoke from their small fire blows away from the direction of Michael and T.J. so they do not alarm the two youngsters.

Michael and T.J. wake up to some of the brisk winds in the area. The sounds of wind whistling through the caves and a cool wind circling around them straight out to the front of the cave shake both of them awake. These winds inspire them to get up and move to the front of the cave and take a good look at the rocky caves that look much different in the daylight hours. The few shallow caves and rock surfaces look part natural and part carved out or cleared out by people. It is still cool this morning, but the sun is shining and the light bouncing off of the smooth rocks make both Michael and T.J. feel surprisingly good.

"Looks like it is trail mix for breakfast, T.J. Then I don't know about lunch." As even her grand amount of trail mix is coming to an end, as they are down to a few handfuls each for breakfast and not much left after that.

T.J. asks the question of the morning, "Well, do we turn back and go back to camp before we run out of food?" The set of open, above-ground caves still is sending the sound of the wind whipping through the caves right at them. T.J.'s hat flies off from a burst of air that comes up from beneath a lower cavern like a geyser blast. She uses some of the water to wash her face, wet her hair, and do some mini-toothbrushing and Michael does the same.

The length to the front of the cave is a short walk of about a hundred feet. The only sound between Michael and T.J. is the strong 'whooshing" sound of wind through the caves. It is a refreshing wind, but not a refreshing sound. The tunnel provides a blast of enthusiasm. They walk out through the cave opening and up a mini rock slope. Almost immediately, they reach another trailhead. They suddenly see it. A sign. It's not out in the distance. It is right in front of them. T.J. says, "Where did that come from? There is no turning back to camp now." They see it. It is the sign from the map!

Chapter 27

They see the Willis sign! After a day of hiking Michael and T.J. finally see a clue that is clearly marked on the last map. Michael's mind instantly opens up like he is laying back on the hammock in 0-80's garage apartment. The sign is standing just out to the right as they exit the cave. The small set of caves and rocky area is not that large, and they go straight over to the Willis sign. Michaels says to T.J. "It was so close, but even the lights from the night sky didn't shine strong enough to see this old beat-up sign." The old but sturdy sign sits just off to the side of their current path.

The sign is on a post about six feet high and it says Willis Trail. Michael pulls the last map out and looks at the secret code and talks about the clues to T.J. She is often good at figuring things out because she isn't really trying to figure anything out. When Michael asks her how she does it, she says, "Well, probably because of how I live life. Unlike the world, I'm not really trying to figure anything out."

Michael laughs and replies, "Ha, nature has really opened up your mind, now you're giving life advice?"

T.J. Says, "I guess so, I believe in unlimited guesses, so no need to figure it out right away." She decides to take a look at the last map and the secret words that have appeared.

"The map says Ron Willis. Who is Ron Willis? I got no clue," T.J. says even after her speech about a life of unlimited guesses.

They both stare at a post with a sign on it that says Willis Trail. "This must be it, Ron Willis trail?" Michael questions. They are looking at it, but the trail goes in three different directions. They both walk up to the sign slowly as if they are coming up on a hidden door. Upon closer inspection Michael is instantly confused. The trail is dedicated to a Nathaniel Willis with a small written plaque towards the base of the sign. "Well then, who was Ron?" T.J. asks the question aloud, as she knew all of the clues from the last map herself.

Michael has a sinking feeling that keeps coming back to him. He instantly thinks of all the trouble they are going to be in, and the danger he has his young cousin in. Not to mention what his mother is going to do to him. Is this last map a trick? There is no Ron Willis. Michael thinks, *0-80's scrambled brain really got me into it this time.*

After hiking through the deepest darkest forest he has ever seen, the first marker he finally sees doesn't match what he needs to make the map real. Is the last map just a fake? There is no phone in hand to do research, no more letters from 0-80, and nowhere else to go. "It is either left, right, or straight ahead," Michael says. Nathaniel Willis trail has three clear directions to go.

For the first time in the entire journey, Michael starts the calculations in his mind to decide exactly how long it will take to turn around and make it back the way they came from. The entire situation now causes Michael to pause. He talks about what could come next to keep the journey going before he calculates their return trip.

"Maybe Nathaniel Willis' trail leads to Ron Willis trail, and then to his son Gilliam's trail. Hopefully, Nathaniel was the grandfather. Then came Ron. Then came Gilliam. His son Gilliam, like the last map said." Michael is speaking under his breath, looking at his options, "Left, right, or straight." He is repeating it over and over, but has no idea which way to turn.

T.J. is getting anxious and excited that they have found any type of Willis, and says, "Nathaniel is probably just a typo! Happens to me all the time in school."

She is full of energy this early in the morning and says, "Let's move!"

Michael says, "Hold on, which way do we move? let me think."

With Michael lost in thought and T.J. full of morning energy, she begins to sing a song that wasn't on her mom's music player. One of the few songs she would sing with her dad 0-80. It isn't actually a song. It is an old military march that they would say together when 0-80 wanted T.J. to burn off some of her kid energy when he was trying to watch a game. It is a cadence that soldiers sing when counting off their marching steps, one step at a time. 0-80 would use this to keep T.J. moving or marching around in circles but not running too far off. T.J. begins out loud:

"Left, Left, Left-Right-Left
Left, Left, Left-Right-Left"

T.J. would march around the yard while her dad smiled at her very coordinated steps as he glanced up from the screen on his phone.

Michael continues asking himself left, right, or straight, trying to think of all of the maps he had seen in his lifetime, hoping to conjure up a note to guide him. T.J. is now marching around in her own circle, continuing her latest song, only a little louder now, as she begins to lift her anxious knees up a little higher, like a soldier, as best as she can. She says the marching words just like soldiers say them, with the emphasis on the right foot to keep all the soldiers in perfect marching step.

"Left, Left - Left - **Right**— Left

Left, Left - Left - **Right**— Left

Left, Left - Left - **Right**— "

Michael's snappy mind clicks as T.J.'S voice and the word she keeps emphasizing dials into Michael's sharp thoughts. There is no Ron Willis. The trail sign said Nathanial Willis because the map was not looking for a Ron Willis, or a Ron Willis sign.

"T.J., I got it! We got it! You did it!"

T.J. says "I didn't do it. I promise I didn't do it."

"No, it isn't anything bad," Michael says, "We figured out the clue on the map. It isn't Ron Willis; now I see it, or I hear it, or you said it." Michael is speaking very hurriedly before he slows down and looks joyously at T.J.

"R means Right. 'Left, Left - Left - **Right** - Left. Left - **Right** - Left.' Right on Willis. Ron Willis is just another clue. R is for Right. That makes the most sense. Not Ron Willis, but R on Willis. R is for Right on Willis Trail! A right on the trail is the instruction from the last map, and off we go!" Michal now has almost full confidence in the map.

T.J. keeps marching. Michael's excitement has him instantly ten steps ahead when she says, "Wait or give me a piggy-back ride," as she stops marching and sprints to Michael to catch up with him. Now they are really on the right path. They are going to follow and find the treasure of the last map.

Chapter 28

The Big H is staring down at his own map. The villains agree they won't catch the two ahead immediately and only continue to follow them for the time being. The Big H is a bit surprised and a bit impressed with the quick morning start from Michael and T.J. and says, "Let them go off again this morning and see how far they get. We will keep on their trail." Even when Michael and T.J. are not in eyesight, The Big H has a map of his own. The map he drew by hand whenever he found a moment to sneak a look at the last map that Michael occasionally slipped out of his pocket and stared at during the week. He also has the same written clues, including the note about Ron Willis, that Michael has. He's taken these from the letters that Michael wrote back and forth with 0—80.

As he walks up to the same Willis trail marker, he does not understand why Michael and T.J. went right on the trail. However, he turns to Miss Visor and says, "I know that they are a smart couple of runts. If they went this way, we will stay on their trail and then take the map when we all get closer to the treasure."

Miss Visor replies, "Yes, it seems like all the kid and his Uncle do is study maps. I bet he could find a treasure out here before Wildman Trapper himself."

The trail is not as treacherous for Michael and T.J. after they turn right on Willis. Occasionally, there are some fallen trees and rocks they must navigate, and once, the trail becomes tight with sudden trees closing in on both sides. Although they are losing energy fast, the next signpost arrives for Michael and T.J. before too long. It peeks through a heavy bunch of trees and is another sign almost identical to the Willis Trail sign. They can see the word Gilliam from where they stand. Although the sign is only a short distance away, it takes a few more minutes to reach it because the brush and forest around the sign is thick. This sign is much less visible than the previous one. The cousins are now far off of any trail they were to remain on. When they finally get up next to the signpost, there is just enough clearing for Michael and T.J. to stand side by side and look up at the writing that says, 'Gilliam Way,' more clearly now. They both see that it points four different ways and let out dueling sighs.

"This is not getting any easier." Michael says as he looks at the last map and at the first two items written. It reads:

1. Ron Willis
2. Son Gilliam

Michael doesn't think that Gilliam is a son of Ron's, because now he knows there is no Ron at all. The R was for right on Willis trail, not the first letter of a name. What is Son Gilliam? The layout of the first words are the same, so "S" on Gilliam makes sense. Michael asks T.J., "Hey, can you march around in a circle for a little while to help with this clue or something?" T.J. is tired and hot under the bright sun and does not march. She sits at the bottom of the signpost to rest.

Chapter 29

Michael decides the S has to mean South on Gilliam. With the sun way up in the middle of the sky, he is having trouble figuring out which way is south. He takes out his compass and begins to see what direction points south. He asks T.J. if she agrees that S means south and she says, "I don't know. If south is the way you are pointing right now, won't that have us going back down in the same direction?"

She ponders for a moment and says, "You think the map is just a joke to get little kids tired so they march up and down the same part of the hill and don't have energy to annoy their parents?"

Michael says, "The last map is real, I am sure of it, one of the smartest maps ever made. He looks at his compass and confirms that south is in the same direction they just came from. "Maybe they are having us backtrack and then come back up the trail another way to prove we really want to earn it."

"I don't know," says T.J. "If we go back, I don't want to

do more hiking today. It might even be dark again before we get back up here, and our food is low. Let's keep going straight ahead."

"Hmm," Michael says quietly. "S, S, on Gilliam, Straight on Gilliam? Not south. South would take us right back to where we started. T.J., I think you did it again!"

T.J. is about to break into a quick chorus of 'Oops... I did it Again!' and stand up to do a mini dance routine. She then stops abruptly and says, "Did what?" Michael says, "Come on," as he grabs her hand and plunges ahead into another area of forest, with an increasingly minimal trail. T.J. says, "Are we sure S means straight into the bushes?" as her small frame is quickly covered in the thick green and brown forest as they walk ahead.

Just as Michael and T.J. disappear, the villains come up from behind and see the Gilliam sign. The Big H realizes quickly they could lose the kid's trail in the thick brush and forest. Michael and T.J. are already out of sight, and it is only the loud behavior of the two that let The Big H and his villainous team know that they aren't too far ahead. The three villains are getting louder now too as they realize the last map is leading to a treasure. Michael and T.J. definitely hear voices now from behind. Michael says, "I knew it. That isn't an animal, someone else may be out here after us and the last map."

The Big H has hiked for years looking for treasure, and he turns to Miss Visor and Little H to say. I know a way around this rough trail that will save us time. We can beat them to a spot up ahead. They have shown us the map is accurate. I wrote down all of the clues they have. Let's go for it now."

Miss Visor adds, "And if we can't figure something out?"

The Big H says, "This far away from camp, we can do whatever we want with the kids. That includes making them talk and tell us the secrets of the map."

The Big H continues his made-up idea, "No one will ever know. It will be so sad that two kids were lost and never found in the wilderness. We will say we spotted them up ahead, but when they saw us, they tried to climb up higher to escape us and had an unfortunate fall. We may even be the heroes that went out looking for them after they ran off against the orders of all supervision."

T.J. hears the voices behind them coming from the direction of the Gilliam Way sign too. She now has a different focus. This fun adventure has turned into a long night, but with no problems because it is just her and her cousin, Michael. This is the way she likes it. Now, even though it is midday they are in the semi-dark of the forest with some strangers chasing them and AuntMom too far away to help. T.J. becomes a bit nervous. Maybe it is the tension, but T.J. hears every sound of crumbling through the leaves and bark and branches on the forest floor.

T.J.'s heart beats heavily as she moves with Michael under the canopy of trees. T.J. shakes with nervousness in her body. She knows it isn't a good idea, but she can't stop herself from flipping on a flashlight she pulls out of the backpack. She points it straight up shining on her face in the dark forest like she is going to tell a scary campfire story and continues to blurt out a song.

T.J. is promptly cut off as Michael throws his hand over her mouth and says, "Cut it." A little sunlight breaks through the forest and continues to light a reflection up on T.J.'s face. Michael is feeling the tension also, and for the first time in over a year slightly raises his voice towards T.J. about singing too much and too loud. "You know there is someone or something behind us. No more from the T.J. song system."

T.J. apologizes and says, "I was nervous and was thinking about AuntMom for comfort and how far away she is. Then I was thinking about my mom for comfort and how she will always be far away. That is when I always think of her singing and remember she used to sing all these songs everyday and dance around our house when it was just me and her. She would dance around with the broom or me as a dance partner. I move better than the broom, she would say."

T.J.'s nerves continue to build, so she just keeps talking. "You know, she taught me to read by reading lyrics to songs, not from books on the shelf or maps like you do. We always had an artist's picture for each download. With Mom gone and Dad in his 'old age'" T.J. says with a look of uneasiness on her face, "the songs are pretty much all the love I have left from my family." Michael let T.J. continue talking all the way through the deep and dark forest, as talking about her mom was calming her down with each word and each forward step.

Chapter 30

The Big H and his crew use the shortcut. The three overtake Michael and T.J. by cutting up and around a forest section on a slender ledge and bunch of jagged rocks. It is a dangerous shortcut, but a successful one for them. For the first time in this event that has gone on for over a full day, this group is now closer to the treasure than Michael and T.J. They move ahead of them on the trail but are still not ahead of them in terms of knowledge of the last map.

Miss Visor, with her slender frame, is able to navigate the ledge and edges around the rocks and make it back to the trail. She is the first to walk ahead and reach a clearing where an area begins to open up to reveal a big, beautiful batch of color-filled flowers. There are small and medium-size berry bushes to the left and the right of this mini-oasis between the high edges and jagged rocks that surround the space.

Quickly, after Miss Visor arrives, The Big H comes up right behind her and begins to survey the scene. It seems like the map has been right so far. "We saw Willis Trail and Gilliam Way. I am not sure how the kids knew the correct turns to make. That Uncle may have given them some extra clues, or there is something special on the map. How else do they keep getting these clues right? Any other kids I know would be crying for their mommies by now."

Miss Visor says, "I bet I can make them cry for their mommies, just wait until I get a hold of them. Especially the little bopping around one!"

The Big H says, focus now, we are here ahead of them, let's keep going. They can stay lost out here forever. Number three on the list says 'Eat Berries.'" He continues, "Look at both number three 'Eat Berries' and then number four 'Cover Beehive.'" The Big H decides now is the time to go for the treasure while they are out ahead of Michael and T.J. "Maybe those two never make it out of that stretch of the forest. We should just move ahead of them from here. We don't need to wait around for kids to push forward."

Miss Visor endorses the action plan by saying, "It looks like one of us will have to eat the berries to attract some bees away from a beehive while the others cover it up?"

The Big H says, "I'm not sure. That could work. I don't have anything better for this clue."

Miss Visor asks, "Do you think the berries are dangerous? The Big H says, "How should I know? I hike and spend a few nights under the stars from time to time, but I bring my own food and cook it. What do you think I do, walk around the forest and make berry sandwiches?"

Miss Visor continues to challenge The Big H, "How do

you not know if the berries are dangerous—you're supposed to be a camp counselor!"

The Big H replies, "I'm supposed to be rich. Not to worry, close to one hundred percent of these darn kids have allergies anyway. I just tell them don't touch or eat anything or they will trigger their allergies or their friends' allergies, and I will have to give them all shots with an EpiPen or else they might all die, ha, ha, ha!" He continues to show his devious side when he adds, "One kid is even allergic to sugar, kids these days, ha! Poor kid… Happy Birthday, kid here is your cake made of brussel sprouts! Ha!" The Big H laughs as he continues to mock the young allergic campers.

He then adds, looking at Little H walking across the meadow toward them. "No, I don't think they are dangerous. I think it is a very good idea." Little H arrives a moment later. Miss Visor tells Little H to eat a few berries as he is still breathing heavy from the climb. The berries are small in size but slightly bigger than a piece of corn. Many of them are a nice red color with a few other colors mixed in. The red ones look like they are most full of juice, almost ready to pop. The Big H explains what he thinks the berries will do, "Eating the berries is the next direction on the map. It be that we eat the berries to give people on the trail an energy boost."

"Some of these trails can be very tough." Miss Visor adds to help convince Little H. "Go ahead, boost away."

The Big H says, "Take a few. We will have water bottles and bug spray at the ready if too many bees come out."

"Come out of where?" Little H asks.

"We have to draw them out with the berries it looks like."

Miss Visor adds, "I don't see any beehives around here. Eat a few berries, and let's see what you attract. It should show us where the beehive is at least."

Little H is skeptical. The berries look foreign to him, so he says, "You go," to Miss Visor. He continues to make his case, "You must be even more tired than me. You got up here real fast. You think it will give an energy boost. Go ahead."

Miss Visor responds, "No, I am fine, I have been up here enjoying the colors and the breeze, my energy is great!" She twists and turns to show off her flexibility and fitness. "Glad you could join us," she adds with a sneer.

She adjusts her visor and picks several berries to hand to Little H. Little H takes half of them in his hand, leaving the other half in Miss Visor's hand and says to her, "At the same time."

The two agree as The Big H says, "Let me move out a bit, and I will look for the beehive so we can follow the next clue when I see it."

He pretends to turn to the side and takes a few giant steps away from them to look for the beehive. In reality, he is squinting through the corner of his eye. He glances over his left shoulder through the strong sunlight to get a look at how these two will stomach the berries and to see where to take cover if a bee attack does come.

"At the count of three," says Miss Visor. They both begin to put the berries up to their mouth, but Miss Visor wraps her berries in a couple of nearby green leaves from a different flower.

"ONE, TWO, THREE." The berries go directly into the mouth of Little H. Although the berries are in her mouth, Miss Visor doesn't chew and only has the leaves that are wrapped around the berries on her tongue. Little H has no leaves to protect his mouth from the directness of the strange berries. He bites down and chews one or two berries and almost immediately turns his face nearly upside down. He twists his lips and then turns blue, purple, and green in that order over the next two minutes. He burps twice and yells and moans and falls over. He looks like he is running because his legs are moving so fast in a full circle, but he is lying on his side holding his stomach, so he is going nowhere.

Miss Visor turns away to take the leaf and the covered berries out of her mouth and rinses her mouth out with water just in case any of the berry juice came close to coming off of the leaves in her mouth. After overcoming the shock of it all, she gets down to Little H's side. He seems to already be swollen to twice the size he was minutes ago, and he seems to be almost done breathing once the moaning stops.

After staying a safe distance away, The Big H walks up to and stands over Little H. He doesn't see much movement as Miss Visor is down by his side about to check for a pulse. Then suddenly, the Little H has another outburst. This time he does stand up, and his legs start moving. He runs around the entire edge of the clearing area and seems to make some pointing noises in the direction of the cliff behind The Big H and Miss Visor. He then finally dashes around one more time zig-zagging left and right and collapses in the middle of the clearing.

Michael and T.J. are still deep in the thickness of the trees. This is definitely the thickest of all the rough forest areas they have been through over the last day and a half of this journey. Despite her belief in Michael and seeing the last map is coming true step by step, T.J. feels very low energy in another dark trap of trees. T.J. even says "Now we are really lost, and I am running out of energy, and my music player is out of power, and we have no more food. No trail mix while on a trail. Talk about bad times."

Michael isn't able to navigate the overgrown trails very well this time and is losing his concentration and he's not even sure with all of the thick trees and high treetops above that he could fly out of there if he had to. They hit a thinner patch of trees and think they are close to pushing through this section of forest. Just then, they both hear a moaning and commotion from someone, but they cannot see anyone where they are in the forest. The sound of someone or something is encouraging and frightening as the moans sound like someone being tortured and seasick all at the same time. They hear what may be another voice. Michael says it first, but T.J. is thinking it as well when he says, "Come on, let's follow that voice. It may be our only way to get out of here, and it sounds like someone is in trouble ahead."

This development is followed by another hopeful comment by Michael "If they have a phone and a signal, we can call for help and call AuntMom and tell her we are okay." T.J. thinks a little more about how a conversation with AuntMom might go after being lost in the woodland forest for more than a day. She offers a comment of her own.

"I'm not calling AuntMom! If we can find a way to get food delivery and some solar-power charging for my music player, we might be better off just living up here from now on than facing what AuntMom is going to do to us."

After a minute or two heading toward the sounds they heard, they begin to see some light shining through the far end of the trees. In another minute of pushing through limbs and branches, they are near the same clearing full of wildflowers and berry patches.

Chapter 31

Meanwhile, the Big H and Miss Visor move Little H and discuss their latest strategy as they move him. "We better wait for the kids to figure this stuff out."

Miss Visor agrees and offers to help move Little H. "Come on, let's drag him over into part of the thick forest."

The Big H says, "I will take care of it. You go hide out on the other side, so we can keep eyes on those two kids from all parts of the clearing." Pulling Little H along with him, The Big H sneaks into the forest in one section just as Michael and T.J. are falling out of another section a few hundred feet away. They arrive at the clearing like a group of kids to a pizza party and spill out into the open air with all smiles and excitement.

They reach the open space where they can stretch out and move freely. The color of the flowers, the sunshine that is now into the late afternoon, and large gusts of air that are moving across the area refresh them both to the point that they start running a little without knowing where they are going.

Michael gets back to the reality of the last map and sits down right in the middle of the clearing and says, "There is nobody here. Are we so tired that we are hearing things?"

T.J. says, "Or are we so deep in the wilderness that bears are dragging things into the woods for quick snacks! I thought I heard something over in that part of the trees" T.J. points to where The Big H is hiding and starts walking towards the trees.

T.J. can not see the Big H unhook the strap holding his gun around his waist when he notices her pointing in his direction. T.J. is not concerned with anything but the open air. However, if she keeps moving closer to The Big H, she will see them both. The Big H knows he will have to keep her quiet. A gunshot would be way too loud and unnecessary, but a quick hit to the side of T.J.'s head would put her down and silence her for sure.

"Let's stop for a few minutes!" T.J. says as she turns back toward Michael to speak to him. "We finally made it to some open space. Stop and look around."

Michael takes an extra moment to look around. The clearing is a medium-size space overall. On one side is where the villains climbed up as a shortcut to beat them there. The jagged rocks continue to go higher and appear to reach the sky. Behind them is the deep dark forest that they just spent so much time and energy to get through. Straight ahead is the clearing and it extends out to make up the beautiful platform meadow they are currently in.

They notice the beauty while standing in the center of all the different parts of nature around them. It feels like they are on a stage with the high rocks serving as balcony chairs. The forest behind them becomes rows of seats in a dark theater. The area is very much like a stage, and they are being watched. They both look at the remaining part of the clearing in the farthest distance opposite the forest. They see what are a dozen or more patches of berries. Right beyond is nothing but a long ledge that drops down to a low valley. It looks like it drops down off the highest building known to man and to certain death.

It is a spectacular piece of nature and would have been a place for a great picnic with 0-80 and AuntMom. Despite knowing they would be in deep trouble, T.J. does wish AuntMom and her Dad were here. Taking a slow look around the entire area, Michael and T.J. do not notice Miss Visor. She is just below the edge by the jagged rocks, as she climbs back down to near where she first appeared and remains hidden.

She whispers to herself, "Get on with it kids. This ain't no field trip. We need to be paid for all this struggle."

The Big H is only a few steps into the deep dark forest, but as thick as the trees are he is completely concealed from Michael and T.J. They focus on the berries as they slowly creep toward the many bright red berries and are once again even further convinced the last map can be solved.

"Eat Berries," T.J. says, "Finally, a direction I can follow. I'm starving. I could eat ALL of the berries. Where should I begin?

Michaels says, "This is number three on the list of the last map. If we complete this one, we will be halfway done with the list!"

T.J. about faints upon hearing this news. "Halfway done? I feel like I am all the way done." She looks at the list again.

1. Ron Willis
2. Son Gilliam
3. Eat Berries
4. Cover Beehive
5. X-Ray Late Day
6. I + Would + Not = Enter

T.J. continues and says, "So we have to eat berries. Get stung by bees. Get an x-ray to make sure the bee stings don't go into our hearts. Then we go against a warning and enter a scary place. That is all." She gives Michael a sideways gaze and then says after thinking about what she has just laid out for both of them.

"Hmm. Okay, well this is tiring and fun to a point, but from the bee stings on, I am not going to enjoy this, am I?"

Michael jumps on the end of the question right away to put a pause on her discouraging talk, "I'm not sure we will really have a chance to finish this, but we are doing great. So we have hope. Yes, I am hungry, too."

T.J. says as a reply, "You can't eat hope, I am going to go and have some of those berries. I wish I had some bread to make some berry sandwiches. What's the use of walking around the forest if you can't make berry sandwiches? We should have brought some bread."

The Big H and Miss Visor are eagerly watching every move Michael and T.J. make in the open clearing and are getting impatient. They know soon others will be out here looking for the two young adventurers. They see Michael and T.J. approach the berries. Michael is surveying the scene and running the clues and the list through his mind.

T.J. is ready to eat. "Shelter. Water. Food. Fire." she says quickly to herself. She recalls that saying from her dad talking about his time in the outdoors. T.J. is rather happy with herself for remembering some main elements for outdoor survival from her dad.

T.J. picks a bunch of berries and calls out the colors as she does. "A lot of red ones here, must be cherry flavored. A few pinkish ones, not sure, but probably pink lemonade or something." She throws a berry up to catch one in her mouth. The first one bounces off her nose. The second one she throws way too high and misses even worse and it hits her in the forehead, leaving a berry stain right in the middle of her head above her eyes.

She tries tossing up two at a time, hoping one will fall in her mouth. However, she sways her neck toward one on the right and is about to chomp down on it when the one to her left distracts her. She pulls her neck back towards that one, missing them both. Not to be discouraged, she then yells out "bank shot" and tosses one off a jagged rock to the side of the berry patch. It hits the rock and bounces back toward her face, just missing her mouth and bouncing off of her chin. She exclaims, "Almost got that one–I could taste it on my lips."

Then she says, "Okay, okay. This time I am serious," and she lines up two berries in her fingers not to throw up in the air and catch in her mouth. She simply lines up the berries high above her head. The berries are pinched between her fingers with her outstretched arm above her mouth to drop the berries straight down directly to the bottom of her throat. It is a can't miss idea, and the berries are on their way to the back of her throat with a simple release.

T.J. says, "Mmmm, mmmm, mmmm, do we call this dinner or lunch? We need to have both!" There is no missing this time. She is ready to catch and swallow the first berry whole as it drops down directly above her, right toward the center of her mouth.

Chapter 32

Michael's back is turned to T.J. He is contemplating what occurred so far on their journey. He spins back around and leaps up with one of his high-knee, flight-taking jumps and bounds across to T.J. He smacks the berries away right before they reach T.J.'s lips. Michael slaps at every berry he can find near her, starting with the hand that is holding berries down by her side. He even wipes off her face, forehead, and around her mouth as she lets go of the other berries from her beat-up hand. T.J. is startled but not enough to have a quick response to Michael's actions.

"What the! You snack stealing son of a biscuit."

"I'm pretty sure eating these berries isn't going to do us any good," Michael tiredly remarks. "The map has directions, not cooking instructions. This can't mean exactly what it says. So far, doing exactly what the map says on the list would have always led us to confusion and being even more lost or hurt!" He issues a statement to T.J. "We have to figure out what the map wants us to do. Remember Ron

Willis. The R was a word starting with "R" and Son Gilliam. The "S" was a word starting with S followed by the word on. The E in Eat has to be a word starting with "E" followed by the word 'at,' hmm? E at... what? We have to make sense of this. E can't mean east if S didn't mean South. E couldn't mean East, could it? East would take us back into the forest." Michael says, again glancing at the compass he pulls from his pocket, "Once again the way they want us to go takes us back or even further off track with these directions."

T.J. says, "This map tells us what to do by not telling us what to do. I'm not very good at remembering to follow directions in the first place."

Michael reassures her and says, "Well you have been good so far. Remember it was you who figured out both the "R" meaning right, and "S" meaning straight."

Michael then changes his tone and briefly sounds like a teacher to T.J. "Hey, T.J. you are right. You are terrible at remembering directions most of the time."

T.J. comes back at Michael's words and says, "I like your pep talks better."

Michael continues, "No, you are terrible at remembering to follow directions, but you have been great with the last map. These are like a strange type of directions and instructions put together. They aren't really directions like telling you what to do. They are more like figuring out a way not to do what someone tells you to, and you are great at that!"

T.J. looks at Michael like she is still waiting for the compliment part of his sentence. Michael continues as he is trying to figure the latest clue, "The map is like detailed information telling you how something should be done or figured out, and we have been good at figuring out our lives for the last year and a half." Michel gives T.J. the additional more supportive comment to send her some inspiration.

"What could E mean? Let's look around. T.J. stay right here; look slowly through the berries. There may be a sign somewhere in these bushes like the Willis and Gilliam signs we saw before. Maybe it got knocked over or taken down. I will look over there by the cliff. You stay over here in this section. Don't get too close. I can see it is a big drop down."

T.J. says, "I want to look with you."

"Not right now," Michael says, it looks dangerous for real. You might get over there and get nervous and start dancing and miss a step and fall all the way down."

T.J. looks up like she just heard the rudest insult ever and says, "I never miss a step."

Michael says, "Well then you must slip a lot!" Michael fakes a blender laugh in T.J. 's direction to give a boost to her spirits for the few minutes they will be apart, searching around separately. T.J. can only smile.

Michael says, "You look over in front. I will go behind to that ledge. Anyway, if I slip, I can fly right back up here!" Michael says as he leaps over a few of the smaller bushes before he slows himself when he sees how far the drop is over the side. He takes a quick glimpse down to a low valley below.

T.J. asks less than a minute later, "How is it going?" already missing her cousin as she is getting more tired and more and more in need of his comfort.

Michael is fully on the other side of the berry patch, and he inches out towards the long ledge before the big drop off. Slowly and cautiously he gets close to the side in a relatively calm manner. It is pretty peaceful, but he is still a few feet from the very edge. To get right to the end of the cliff and feel safe, he bends down on one knee and goes a foot closer out on a short stone ledge. He then gets fully on his stomach to slowly crawl to the very end to ensure the forceful gusts of wind that are now coming across the open space don't blow him off to take flight. He then inches further and further out. His head is slightly over the ledge as the wind comes up from the valley and feels inspiring.

His eyes are closed as he keeps inching out a bit further. He is imagining a great lift off into flight from so far out on this dangling ledge. He feels miles away from the dark forest and jagged rocks of the past two days. Michael is now so far over the end that he can feel the wind up around his neck and shoulders as he is lying over the ledge, and his upper body begins to slant downward little by little without him even noticing.

Part of Michael's mind tells him, this may be the time for him to show everyone that he can fly. He is reaching a point where he is going to have to fly. He will soon have no choice. His weight is leaning forward, and he looks like he might slide towards the open air and glide down to the harsh rocks below. Michael thinks he can do it, and his momentum is only seconds away from a dangerous point that will take him over the side where fly or fall will be his only two options.

"Hey! Are you at the end yet?" TJ yells to Michael, as she can't see him clearly through the berry bushes and can't see how far out toward certain death he is. T.J.'s voice awakens Michael. His eyes pop open and he looks to his left and right at the lower valley as his eyes get wider and wider as his eyebrows raise high on his forehead. The view of the open valley gives his entire body and mind a boost of motivating imagery. He scoots back a few inches as he realizes how far out on the rock he is. He says to himself, "Just like when I am going to fly," to remember the wind gusts and peacefulness he felt in those brief moments. Then he screams to T.J. "Come here! Be careful. Crawl over on your hands and knees, but you have got to see this." He pauses to add, "Teeeeeeee Jayyyyyyyyyy, we are going to do it!"

Chapter 33

T.J has made it through the large outcropping of berries right before the actual ledge that Michael has gone way too far out on. Michael says, "T.J., get down even lower on your stomach like me. Hold on to me, I know I can fly. Everything will be all right."

T.J.'s nervousness and Michael saying, 'hold on to me' is enough to move T.J. to song. Her voice is cracking now as she is near the cliff, but she still manages most of the opening acapella to En Vogue's Hold On before Michael moves back a bit more so he can reach T.J.'s hand.

T.J.'s song list and ratings:

Hold On

- Music 4 stars, it is booming, but low enough to let all the voices come through
- Singer(s) 5 stars, how many angels can sing on one song!

- Mom Meaning: <u>Hold on to your friends and loved ones.</u> You don't know when they won't be there. -I can hear mom saying that. -She was too right about that one :(

They remain on their stomachs for safety right in front of the ledge, but not nearly as far out as Michael was. As the two lie there like they are lying next to each other back at home, a return to that connection is felt, and they both feel like, despite the entire horribly crazy year or more they have been facing, everything will end up all right.

They scoot back even a bit more as Michael feels T.J. is not comfortable this close to the cliff end and being this high up. Moving back allows Michael to change to a bit more casual mindset. T.J. calms down a bit. It really is a beautiful view of the valley below.

She says they are even so high up and the cliffs go so far down, "I would skydive from here."

Michael feels her calm, "I can fly. No need for skydiving for me, but here is the thing about skydiving everyone else who can't fly needs to know." He tells T.J., "This is a tip for you and all of your skydiving friends." He says jokingly, "You don't even need a parachute to go skydiving."

"You don't need a parachute to go skydiving?" T.J. says, "What!" He then pauses unable to hold back a smile before he delivers his next line to T.J.

"You only need a parachute if you want to go skydiving TWICE!" This gets a glorious blender laugh from T.J. that echoes off the jagged rocks down below the canyon to the valley floor, creating a chorus surrounding them with the wondrous humor they always share.

They both slowly look around from out on the furthest rock ledge they are lying down in front of. Now T.J. sees it too. First, a crystal-clear lake that doesn't appear to be that deep. It is dried up to what must be less than half of its original size. What remains of the lake is like a beautiful piece of clean glass. Michael explains that they must still get some snow or moisture at the high elevations off the jagged rock cliffs, and the water runs down and fills in that low area. It feels cooler down there as well based off all of the wind whipping by us on this ledge.

Michael says to T.J. "Now scoot out just two more inches with me and look beyond the lake. What do you see?"

T.J. says it like she doesn't believe it herself. "I see a beehive!" comes from her voice, but it is more of a squeaky excitement than her normal voice. Slowly but happily she begins to even feel her cheeks perk up with a smile even while out far on the long edge. "I see a bunch of beehives!" She now feels the last map in her soul.

From the ledge, they can see past a large set of jagged rocks that jump up to block the view of the lake and beyond for anyone who isn't at least this far out on the ledge beyond the berries. There is a series of rolling and twisting mounds in the distance that rise out of the ground that look just like beehives. Beyond the beehives, there is another set of trees. Another forest that is pushed back a little more than a few hundred feet from the beehive mounds.

T.J. says, "This is our lucky day. We must be meant to complete the last map. We found the beehive and didn't even use the clue."

Michael cuts in, "Yes we did get to use the clue. We had to use the clue. The beehive, you couldn't see it behind the high jagged rocks unless you went all the way through and to the other side of the berry patch, to the rock ledge above the canyon. To the very edge. Eat Berries, E at Berries, E for Edge. Edge at Berries. Edge at berries." T.J. and Michael both move back farther from the cliff toward the berry patch on solid ground. T.J. stops to get Michael back for saying that she would ever miss a dance step as she remembers that dig from her cousin.

She spins around like a top and starts to dance by rocking back and forth, singing another song. She jokes with Michael, "Hey, you finally got a clue too. Thanks for helping out the team!" The remark comes from a spinning, grinning youngster who first loses her hat flying off her head while spinning around. Then does a cartwheel towards the middle of the meadow that would not be on beat with any music or song no matter what she was signing. She then does slip and fall. She hits the soft ground of the grassy meadow. As she lies there looking up at the sky she thinks, *how many songs will I have to sing to keep me going to get to those beehives?*

Part IV

Chapter 34

Michael and T.J. realize there are "beehives" that they have to cover. They see where they need to go. The question is, how far and how long will they have to travel to get down and over to the beehive mounds? They are already exhausted, and they hear things behind and around them. T.J. is far away from the ledge in the middle of the clearing. She finally decides to stand up and rises, wobbling like she is light-headed.

Once she gets both feet on the ground and appears stable, T.J. says to Michael with great feeling, "I think we have to make it to the finish line of the last map." She puts her hand on her hip as Michael is now the one gaining inspiration from her. T.J. continues, "Let's do it together like the family we are."

"Like the family we need." Michael adds quietly as the center of the meadow has gone silent from any gusts of wind for the moment.

They nod at each other in agreement. The two are now both fully re-engaged in the mission.

Michael says, "I saw something else on the ledge. Follow me."

This time with no thick forest in front of them, Michael is leading the way confidently. He cuts across the meadow in front of the berry patch. T.J. is moving well and keeping up with him. Michael is lying on the ledge out in the open-air, and it gives him a unique view. He shares that view with T.J., "I saw a small stairway trail carved into the rocks that would have been hidden unless you were out almost as far as I was. The stairs are more like small footholds. There are probably a hundred of them carved into the rocks."

Michael and T.J. follow a path to the side of the trail to the rock footholds that are hard to see. Stretching around the rounded rock, they are able to reach the first foothold. It is a series of steps that they can take with little difficulty. They step up and then wind down a few feet to a slide that looks like it is naturally carved out of smooth rock.

There is also a direct path that is a lot easier to walk on that leads to a place above the foothold path they have chosen. Both paths seem to go up first and then lead to carved-out rockslides that go down quite far. Michael sees a small amount of moisture on the smooth rock surface going down. It looks like they were carved out of thousands of years of water cutting through this part of the trail. The slide Michael and T.J. are closest to goes down far. They can't see where it ends. The slope seems to be almost all naturally made. Still, the stairs have been carved or chiseled out to make it easier to get to this natural passageway.

T.J. says, "Oh, chutes and ladders, I like this part of the map's plan. The Buffalo Soldiers made a playground slide to bring some fun to this journey. Smart map. They should have made treasure hunting apps!" She says it like it is a million-dollar idea. "Maps not Apps!" Michael says, channeling his best 0-80 old man tone.

Chapter 35

They both reach a stillness as it is mesmerizing to look at the smooth rock sloping down along with the natural sandstone and darker colors in the rock. T.J. and Michael don't see any bottom to the slide at all. They toss a few pebbles down to make sure this isn't another wrong direction that ends badly for whoever makes the mistake.

The pebbles don't slide at first. They bounce and ping and rattle at the top before they make their way down. Toward the middle of the slide the pebbles start to evenly run along the rock face. They see the pebbles come out of the tunnel end of the slide and down onto a slightly sloped end of the ride. T.J. questions, "Should we go over to the easier trail and try that slide? That didn't sound like a VIP ride to me." Michael says, "No, this is the way I could see from the edge at the berries. The other path wasn't even visible. This should be a fun ride after the first bumpy part." He quickly adds, "let's ride down on our backpacks to cushion the slide." T.J. remarks sadly, "They are pretty empty anyway, I have been out of supplies for a while, and we are low on water in that pack."

As the two cousins huddle together at the top of the slide, they move closer to the very beginning of the slope. It seems to go more straight down than it did before when they tested it out with the pebbles. Michael sits right at the top of the slide on his empty backpack. T.J. takes a more cautious approach and sits on the empty water pack first and then scoots forward up near the top of the slide.

Michael and T.J. let out a big breath together. They take smaller quick breaths and then they both sit with their legs in the perfect position to slide down. Michael says, "One, two, threeeee." On three he pushes himself forward out of T.J.'s arms, thinking that she is going to move forward on three also.

Michael is gone immediately. He is already partially down the slide when he hears T.J. continue to count. "Four, five, six, seven…" Michael slides down on his backpack in a bumpy fashion but a nice constant speed. The amount of wind whipping in his face and around his body is much stronger than the average slide.

The wind from the canyon floor is funneling up and through each of the rock faces and slide tunnels. Michael adjusts to the blast of air, and then it hits him. T.J. has not come down the slide. He looks back over his shoulder to double confirm that she is not coming. He begins to try and stop himself. However, he is at the smoothest part of the rock face and slides down at an even stronger pace. Finally, the curve begins to level out, and he comes to a light tumbling stop at the end of the slide without T.J. anywhere near him.

Chapter 36

H e stands immediately at the bottom of the slide. For the first time in the entire journey Michael is truly panicked. T.J. is not by his side, not traveling with him, not singing or humming a song as a soundtrack to their always outrageous activities. He starts to try to climb back up the slide but slips down, once, then twice.

He stares back up at the slide from his knees. He looks at the steep slope and smooth rock and knows that it is not climbable. He stands and says to himself while looking up at this obstacle, "This definitely is unclimbable, but it is not unflyable." This is the time that Michael Jefferson must fly. He will race back up the cliffside in protection mode for his cousin. There is no time for a 3, 2, 1 countdown. Michael needs to simply explode into the sky to save his family, like a hero exploding off of the pages of maps he knows so well.

He plants his feet and bends down deeply until he can feel the energy in his knees. He feels the energy in his soul. Michael Jefferson, the boy who thinks he can fly, looks straight up into the sky and bends down even farther ready to boost up high. He powers his legs and then his chest. His chin gains strength as he glances up even higher. Michael then starts to raise high up off of his toes. As he elevates off the ground, he feels the triumph in his legs.

His legs are surprisingly light. He knows this is how it feels to fly. Suddenly, as he feels air under the soles of his shoes, his feet are slammed out from under him. A rolling stumbling happily screaming T.J. comes down the slide just at the moment of his launch to take flight. She hits the bottom of the slide and rolls into Michael right above both his ankles. He falls over forward, and T.J. tangles up with Michael as they both lie on the smooth rocks at the bottom of the slide.

T.J. gets up first, as Michael is both happy and mad that he was taken out by T.J. She rises and says while looking at Michael, "Everyone knows you don't stand at the bottom of a slide. I learned that in Pre-K. What else do you do in your spare time? Jumping jacks on railroad tracks?" She begins to laugh with her rhyme. Michael says, "What happened to one, two, three?" T.J says, "I counted to ten and then did a countdown back down from ten, 10, 9, 8, 7, 6, 5, 4, 3, 2, 1, blast off! I thought that is what we were doing."

"No," Michael says, "Blast off is when you go up and fly! We were going down, 3,2,1, go! That is pretty much known all over the world. You should have learned it in Pre-K."

"Well, is it 1, 2, 3, or 3, 2, 1. I think you are even confusing yourself now." T.J. pauses to consider the different countdown strategies. Michael is already over his brief anger with his cousin and turns his focus back to the last map. He sees a few more small steps or descending footholds all the way down to the cavern floor that lead directly to the beehive mounds.

Chapter 37

On the cavern floor there are more strong gusts of wind. The winds whip in, around, and toward the beehive-like mounds. Fortunately, it is a helping wind at Michael and T.J.'s backs. It even pushes them forward a bit. This continues to encourage them past exhaustion to reach the beehives. The Big H and Miss Visor are stuck up above and behind them. Miss Visor is still hiding out below the rock stairs where Michael and T.J. slid down. She doesn't see where the slide starts, and she doesn't hear them speaking with the wind blowing through the rockslides. The woman is now more angry as she misses the exact path they slid down. She knows they slid down to the bottom but is confused by the route they took to get there.

Miss Visor climbs up to near where Michael and T.J. were to investigate. She stops at the round rock. Without being over on the berries' edge, the stone stair holds blend in with the natural rock. It is beyond difficult to see the little holds on the far side of the round rock leading to the rock-slide Michael and T.J. used. There is a wider path much

easier to see and follow, but it leads to different rock formation slides.

Miss Visor makes her way back over to the meadow
with all of her new information trying to think what to do
next. To her surprise, as she reaches the meadow to discuss
strategy with The Big H, he and Little H are there to greet
her. The Little H is still looking sick and hunched over. Miss
Visor takes her time to report how she believes Michael and
T.J. have made their escape down the rocks and have again
moved in front of them. While she reports her findings and
observations, The Big H drags Little H forward. The Big H
is almost drowning him in water all over his face and neck
to revive him to a normal state.

The Big H says to Little H, "Wake up. It is time to go
for a ride," and gives a sideway glance. Miss Visor helps to
slowly and carefully walk him over to the rock slide area.
They begin to follow the wider path up. They help or push
Little H up the short trailway. They walk right past the
round rock and small footholds and are left with two other
options.

They are looking at two possible slides. Which one leads
to the bottom and which one leads somewhere else, like off
the side of the cliff? The Big H pushes and moves Little H
toward one of the slide openings. Little H tries to push back
a bit. He is in a weak state from his berry-eating sickness.
Miss Visor rushes in and wraps her claw-like hand and
strong grip around his arm and steers him to the slide
opening.

Little H tries to object to the decision, but as he tries to
speak, he coughs up another berry seed from his stomach
that is now stuck in his throat. He even looks to be swelling

up again. The coughing is getting louder and forceful now and coming from high above. The coughs are a deep barking noise. The sound echoes down and around the valley below. Michael and T.J. are on their way to the beehive mounds. Michael hears the sound and turns back quickly and sees flashes of three people high above them. They are behind some of the rocks. He can't identify who they are. However, he sees they seem to be struggling with each other. He continues to look back as he is walking forward and sees a horrible sight.

The Big H and Miss Visor take the opportunity of Little H bending over and coughing furiously to send him barreling down the rockslide. This is not the slide that Michal and T.J. chose. This secondary slide starts off as a bouncy ride like the route Michael and T.J. took. Unlike the cousins' route, the one taken by Little H does not level out to a smooth stop. It goes from bouncy to rocking and rolling, and it only gets worse from there.

Little H goes pummeling down, down, down. The end of the ride is the opposite of a soft, smooth landing. The rockslide comes to a sudden end twenty-five feet above the ground. Little H bounds out of the slide tube straight down with a loud crunch. Michael does not alert T.J. to what he sees. She is humming along to a few songs but looking very tired and is not paying much attention. Once Michael sees the terrifying fall, he speeds up and pulls T.J. along faster with him as she struggles to keep up.

Miss Visor says coldly, "Tough flight, tougher landing," as Little H is not moving at the bottom of the rock base and doesn't look like he will be moving anytime soon. The Big H looks down and sarcastically proclaims, "We will spend your share of the treasure in your honor," before he turns his attention to a deep discussion about the other rockslide that appears before them.

Miss Visor says, "I don't know; we could be missing something here. I would go down the other slide, but I really don't want you to make a speech about spending my part of the treasure in my honor. The kids must have some additional information on that map. We just need to take it from them and be done with it."

"I agree with both points. This is too risky," The Big H says. "We can climb down. I have the gear in the bag. We catch up with them and take it." Miss Visor hesitantly nods her head up and down in confirmation of the plan. She is confident they can overtake Michael and T.J. She replies with a devious tone.

"We just caught them. We made it in front of them. If we climb down with speed, we can get them again, and soon!"

The Big H says, "These kids can move, and they are slick. Like you said, we are done chasing them to catch up with them. We are going to overtake them and take them out." He nods his head up and down back at Miss Visor and lowers his eyebrows, showing the intensity of his words. "We will finish the map ourselves. With our skills and abilities, the curves and turns from the map won't stop us. We have to be getting close to the treasure. We will catch those two small-timers and tear every inch apart, and turn over every leaf of this area to find our treasure, or beat the information out of them before we dispose of them if that helps our cause."

Chapter 38

M iss Visor and The Big H work very well together as
they use a series of ropes and hooks and make it
halfway down the dangerous side of the cliff quickly. Miss
Visor's thin strong frame helps her move down ahead of
The Big H. He is moving just fine himself until a slight slip
of his left foot makes him suddenly grip a rock with the full
might of his hands.

This gets a cackling laugh from Miss Visor as she looks
up to see The Big H sliding with his feet on the smooth
rock for a few moments until he regathers himself. She
stops laughing when The Big H, kicking against the side of
the cliff, sends some rocks down toward her and below to
the ground. Her cackling laugh turns into a screech or two.
This noise along with the small and medium-size rocks
popping down on the ground are enough to alert Michael
and T.J. They are continuing forward and have almost
reached the beehive mounds.

Michael sees the two climbing down and is surprised to
see how fast they are moving. Michael quietly alerts T.J. of

the two people he sees peering down at them. "Come on T.J. We really have to move." T.J. says, "Wait, is that a rescue party? Maybe they have food." Michael immediately rules the villains out as a rescue party. He knows they are not friendly to their mission.

Michael tells T.J. about the man he saw them push down the rockslide. "I don't think he is ever going to be heard from again." He emphasizes his claim. "They aren't here to rescue us. They would have called out to us as soon as they saw us. They would have been calling out for us even before they could see us in the forest. I'm sure they are after us or after the last map."

Michael continues looking up at them on the side of the cliff as they move down toward the bottom of the canyon to chase them on foot. Just then, he sees a strong ray of sunlight cut across the sky, and it reflects right off of the front of Miss Visor's actual visor. It hits Michael directly at that moment. He realizes who is climbing down after them. "The Big H and Miss Visor, that's who they are." T.J. says, "That Big H wasn't ever friendly to me. How were The Big H and Miss Visor to you?" Before Michael can answer, T.J. thinks back over the last week and says "Miss Visor always tilted her Visor down to cover what she said when I looked at her talking with the Big H. And I think she tried to scare me one time just for her own enjoyment."

What started out as a quest to follow the last map is now also a quest for survival and escape. Michael looks up to judge how close the two villains are as they near the bottom of their climb. He is too far away to lock eyes with The Big H, but there seems to be heat coming out of his stare. He can see they are not new to climbing and knows they are strong hikers. It is only a matter of time before they catch up with him and T.J. He shifts his eyes over to look at Miss Visor. She is even closer to the bottom than the Big H and even more visible. The anger in Miss Visor's stance on the rock wall tells him that this isn't going to end well. He warns T.J., "It doesn't look like they will get tired anytime soon before they catch up to us. Keep moving. We are almost there now."

Chapter 39

Now that they see they are being followed, Michael and T.J. find another reserve of energy to run. How long were these villains behind them? They make it to the beehive mounds in half of the time they were expecting. Once they reach the front of the mounds, they both stop and look up and are breathing very fast from their sudden sprint. Neither of them moves ahead any further. Michael takes the time to uncover the last map and really study it for the thousandth time as he tries to breathe evenly.

The cousins need to keep moving forward, But they have not figured out what to do. They use the minute it takes to catch their breath to recharge through their special connection. They are happy to have a friendship that maintains over time, space, and circumstance. They are transformed from this two-day continuous journey to a fun-loving bubble of friendship.

Michael says out loud to no one in particular, "This is an odd list, for odd days, from an odd uncle, in an odd family."

T.J. adds, "a very odd list."

Michael adds, "Abnormal even." They have completed half of the tasks. This gives the two permission to be a little reflective and momentarily playful about the journey they have been on.

T.J. says in reply to the word abnormal from Michael and challenges him by saying, "So, you have another big word to describe our days?"

Michael thinks for a moment and says, "Quirky."

T.J. says, "Okay, I have no idea what that is, but I have one. 'Wacko'!" as she bounces around so happy with herself like they are back walking down the street to their tired house on the way home from school.

The joking bubble of friendship doesn't pop suddenly, but it slowly drops away when they both hear Miss Visor slip on a rock. They are pulled back into the drama of the situation immediately.

Miss Visor slides down the final ten feet of her climb. Then she unintentionally does a backflip on the way down and athletically lands on her feet before she does a full turn and tumbles over on her face. This causes her visor hat to come off. Her face and body are scratched up from this cool but awkward move. This is beyond funny to Michael and T.J. as they watch in the far distance across the canyon. Miss Visor is enraged. One of her buns has fallen completely out. She is trying to inspect the damage she has taken on, and stands up and looks like something out of a scary movie; one side of her hair still in a bun and the other side of her long hair hanging down near her waist towards the ground.

T.J. says, "From bun head to spun head, not her best

look," and laughs at the top of her lungs which makes Miss Visor more mad as she stares intensely across the canyon floor. She can't see the two in detail. She can only see two smaller specs of people and hear a strangely big laugh echoing out around her. The Big H is only a few moments from completing his climb down and standing beside her.

Chapter 40

"We lose them in the mounds," Michael exclaims. The mounds are amazing to look at. They seem to bubble up from the ground right in front of them. "Rock and clay," Michael says as he touches the first big mass of raised earth in front of the others. The brilliant color of the sandstone mounds reflect the evening sun.

Michael peers through the mounds. Some are spaced out by more than a few feet between each one, but most paths between them are narrow. Other mounds grow together and block off a route of passage entirely. They vary in height. Some of the bigger ones that got Michael's attention from far above are nearly fifty feet high. Looking at them up close, they see most of the mounds are ten to twenty-five feet tall. Over a hundred mounds link together in this area of nature.

The rounded masses are more than high enough for Michael and the minuscule T.J. to hide behind. They jog in and make a few quick twists and turns among the maze. They notice multiple paths through the "beehive mounds."

They try two different routes. One of the paths leads to a stop where two of the bigger mounds come together. Michael and T.J. turn around and go back to the front of the network of nature made paths.

The second attempt crisscrosses and takes them back to the beginning of this obstacle course. Each time they come back out to the front of the mounds, they see the villains magnified as they are coming closer and closer across the canyon floor. The last time they emerge from the mounds the villains are close enough to see their hateful expressions in full detail. The Big H and Miss Visor are jogging straight down toward them, only to be slowed by the packs on their backs. They look so mean and so determined it makes T.J. say aloud. "I wish they were bears."

Michael and T.J. duck back behind the beehive mounds. This time they do not follow any path. They go deep enough to stop and study the last map for some clues. "Look at the last map. It hasn't failed us yet," Michael reminds T.J. as they both study the list on the map.

1. Ron Willis
2. Son Gilliam
3. Eat Berries
4. Cover Beehive
5. X-Ray Late Day
6. I + Would + Not = Enter

The mid-day sun is now another of the many memories of the already long journey. It is gone and is part of a day that seems to be draining the life out of T.J.'s legs with each passing minute. It is almost two full days out here. Without saying a word to each other, they both know they won't make it through a third day.

Looking at the map, they start to consider what the clues could mean.

"T.J., What do you think?" Michael asks.

T.J. answers, "I'm too hungry to reply. Shouldn't a beehive have some honey somewhere?"

Michael reminds T.J. of the serious situation. "Treasure or no treasure, we have to stay ahead of The Big H and Miss Visor." T.J. tries to gather her brain power and says, "Well, before the crazy days of our adventure, and the tricky clues before, if you think about it, we would have covered up the beehives."

T.J. continues, "We seem to do the opposite sometimes and it works out better than really following the clue. We uncover the beehive, and then get the treasure and get out of here." T.J. is talking in long, drawn out, unfocused answers now.

"I don't think this is where the treasure is because there are two more clues after this one. I like the opposite part of it, to uncover the beehive," Michael says as he cuts in and tries to bring some focus to their ideas. "I don't really know if that works like the others. The action wasn't even the actual clue before."

He looks at T.J. and sees how drained she is and feels he needs to address her food question, "T.J., sorry there won't be any honey. But if we can get through this and keep moving, we have a little water. We have always been able to find more water." To try to end on a positive note, he adds. "We can figure it out, T.J."

"I don't know. We can't get this one and they are

coming for us. If we have to do something to uncover it, should we start to dig? With what?" T.J. is now talking and questioning herself. She is so worn out.

Michael and T.J. know that the last map does not give clues to follow directly. Following the clues word for word usually has someone going right back the way they came or worse. "They are directives or actions, secret ones, with hidden meanings," Michael keeps reminding himself.

T.J. says, "Very hidden."

"We are hidden for now." Michael says to bring some comfort. "But they are fast and are sure to be coming up to the beehives very soon."

"What are we going to do when we can't hide in here anymore? We don't want to bump right into them going around the beehives." T.J. peeks around the side of the mound to see how close the villains may be.

Michael decides, "Get up on one of these mounds. We still have water, not much, but we have some. They won't see us up there. Let's refresh, refuel, and figure out how to make our escape. Maybe discovery isn't what we are trying to do now. This may only be a survival trip at this point."

T.J. quickly and smartly asks, "Speaking of survival, we never confirmed that there aren't any giant bees inside?" Michael assures her that there are not any bees inside, although with how the last two days have gone, how can he really be sure?

Chapter 41

The two have to assist each other to get to the top of one of the taller beehives with a series of push and pulls between them. Some of the sides have a few places to grip, but it is a struggle to reach the top of a tall beehive mound.

"Ugh, err, ugh,"

"You're pulling on my neckbone."

"I am pulling you up by your collar. Grab my arm. There is no neckbone."

"Well then how does someone break their neck?"

"They break bones in their neck, but they don't break one singular neckbone. You are talking about your collarbone."

After they make it to the top of the mound, they can see more standing up, but they both scrunch down to not be visible to anyone below, like the Big H or Miss Visor. The villains reach the beehives and begin to run through the crisscross trails, looking for Michael and T.J.

Number four on the list from the last map, "Cover

Beehive." No answer to this part of the puzzle comes to mind. Both Michael and T.J. look up and around them hoping for a clear way out of this predicament. All they see is another big set of trees beyond the beehives. They do not look forward to going in that direction. They know they will not make it through another long forest hike.

It is harder to think about the clues and figure out what to do next when they are being followed and chased. Michael has a small sip of the last round of water. "Take some big drinks and finish off the last of it," he says as he hands it to T.J.

Michael steadies himself and his mind as his thoughts always seem to bounce back and forth between dealing with the situation at hand or flying away to a safer place. He settles somewhere between the two. Flying away in his mind gives him enough space and mental room to come racing back and deal with a real situation at hand. This has always been his way.

The real situation becomes frighteningly real as he hears The Big H and Miss Visor somewhere very nearby. They may even be directly below them as they hear them wandering through the beehive mounds talking about what they can cover them with. Their clothes? Their ropes? They are unsure and frustrated and Michael and T.J. hear them begin to go through their packs.

Michael whispers, "If we stay up here long enough and stay down low enough, they won't see us, and they will probably think we have gone somewhere else. They will walk right by and then we can make our escape." Michael's words bring another quiet song to T.J.'S lips as she begins to sing Dionne Warwick's "Walk on By." Michael says, "hey, I like that song, but sing quietly, T.J. I know you are nervous, but quietly under your breath."

T.J. stops singing and says, "Of course you like it. It is a great song. It is like saying you like a sunset. Who doesn't like a sunset?" Luckily, the noise and commotion the villains are making emptying out their gear to try and cover a beehive mound is loud enough that Michael and T.J. are not heard.

T.J.'s song list and ratings:

Walk on By

- Music 5 stars: it is like cool jazz type of sad and happy music put together
- Singer 5 stars: she sounds smooth
- Mom Meaning: About walking by people you don't like and minding your business and they mind theirs. How it should be. - I can hear mom saying that.

Michael calls his attention to the actual sunset that is still above the horizon in the distant sky. He takes a moment to look at it. He has a bit of relief as although he can't see, he can definitely hear The Big H and Miss Visor, furiously trying to set up some kind of covering for a beehive mound with their tarps and sleeping bags and ropes far across from them. As they start their construction and begin to build up the side of a mound, Michael can now see a bit of what they are attempting.

"It looks like they are trying to build a skyscraper with popsicle sticks and paper towels," he reports to T.J.

"There is steam coming off of both of them from their anger." The Big H and Miss Visor have set up a difficult base and are trying to get some of the sleeping bags to cover the beehive mound. It looks like it will take them some time.

Michael continues to watch the sun starting to cast long shadows on the ground. He glances over toward a row of four trees that are fifty feet out in front of the intimidating forest. From up where he is sitting, they look like four doormen standing in front of a great big high-rise hotel. At ground level, the four smaller trees blend into the huge forest behind them although they are planted out in front of the huge trees. From up above on the beehive, the higher perspective shows the first four trees clearly out in front.

This set of four trees on the outer edge of the beehive mounds are now being studied by Michael. He remains frozen in place trying to get a plan to come to mind. There isn't much else to look at in any direction from atop the beehives. Behind them is the canyon they ran across to get to the mounds. There are the rock walls from the high cliffs that go up around the canyon. The beehive mounds are otherwise surrounded by more and more forest and trees. Into the trees was really the only way forward. The trees go from side to side covering Michael's field of vision.

Michael says, "Look at those four smaller trees out in front of the larger forest behind."

"Not more trees, do I have to look?" In her hungry and tired state, T.J. can only find the energy to say, "I already don't like vegetables. Now I never want to see anything green for the rest of my life." T.J. starts to squirm in place, thinking about the scratches down on her legs from the last forest they marched through.

The trees are so big Michael can't see how deep this forest is. He knows that running into another big, dense, deep forest with a lack of food and water could really lead to a situation of never being heard from again. They are lying flat on their stomachs, thinking about going ahead into another forest that they do not have the energy to run into. Neither of them says a word to each other because they are out of moves to make. T.J. rolls over on her back and looks up at the sky. Michael doesn't know what else to do, so he does the same. They are so tired; both of them close their eyes. Too tired to sing. Too tired to fly. This time no answers come to Michael's mind.

Chapter 42

The wind picking up through the beehive mounds and noise from the villains awakens them. Michel and T.J. both come alive from a few brief moments of sleep that has helped them gain a bit of energy. Michael picks his head up and peeks to see The Big H and Miss Visor have a structure that looks surprisingly well built. If they stand on the structure and reach the top of their beehive, they will easily look across and see them. T.J. now looks over at the villain's strong construction and sadly realizes what they must do. "Into the forest we go again." After a pause, she adds, "maybe I can't this time."

They scout out the two right turns and one left it will take to make it to the trees from where they are. They slide down the mound together. Michael tries to take off in a tired sprint when he reaches the ground. He instantly slows to make sure he does not leave T.J. behind. They are not seen by The Big H or Miss Visor. They escape the beehive mounds unnoticed for now and head for the trees.

Michael and T.J. stand side by side like cardboard cutouts. There is almost no animation left in their undersized bodies. They look even smaller facing another giant obstacle. They are staring at the four front trees next to each other with the larger forest less than one hundred feet beyond the front trees.

Michael considers what will happen if they dive into another forest trail. He studies the forest like he is asking the trees a question. He looks at the first four trees that are getting hit with sunlight from the setting sun behind them. The trees serving as doormen now look more like guards. The first tree is short and stubby. The next one is even more stout than the first but a bit taller overall. The third one is unlike the first two. A few feet up its tree, the sturdy trunk splits in two directions like the letter "v". It looks like one road on a highway slowly separating into two. The fourth tree is big but slimmer and still looks very strong. Michael looks at all four as if he needs to ask them permission to go into the dark realm behind them.

He even nods at the trees as he passes between the two middle trees with T.J. right behind him. He reaches his arms out and touches the bark on the strong tree on his right and pats the tree with the split tree trunk at its base on his left. He notices a thin black wire keeping the two sides of the split tree trunk in place.

It appears the four guardian trees let them pass, and they are on their way across the short clearing to the set of big trees. Both hesitate to go in. They turn and look back at the setting sun. They know the darkness that these heavy forest trees bring even in the daytime and evening is here as the sun continues a slow descent across the wilderness sky.

"We have to make it to the dense part of the trees again

and try to lose them there. We have lost them before, and we will do it again." Michael is trying to convince both T.J. and himself. Neither wants to move as they start walking closer to the forest. They know soon they will have to worry about what it is like to be in the forest at night. T.J. says to herself and to build up their spirits, "Well, we almost made it. We finished half of the last map."

Michael agrees and tries to boost their spirits even further. "We did make it halfway through the map. If we can survive this, and the trouble we will be in for the next twenty years, maybe we can return when we are grown-ups and finish the last map. We made it through one, two, and three on the last map! We can always be happy about that."

Michael looks at the map one last time. He sees four, five, and six. Four is still a mystery, Cover Beehive, "We had to escape instead of deal with that."

"At least we escaped," T.J. tries to get to the bright side of their failure.

"Five is X-ray late day. No other clue was written like that. Who knows how long it will take to figure that out. It could be a whole 'nother mystery."

"Don't forget about six!" T.J. knows he hasn't forgotten it but wants to make sure he is extra cautious even talking about it.

"Six is a warning." Michael thinks out loud,

"Maybe it is best we didn't make it to number six!"

They have reached the very front of the big heavy forest. He turns around and looks back at the four guardian trees and scans out past the beehive mounds to look at the setting sun one last time before they plunge into forest darkness as he reaches down to grab T.J.'s lonely hand.

T.J. is facing the forest with her head pointed up toward the big trees and pulls out enough strength to say, "We can't."

Michael still looks back toward the clearing at the four guardian trees and the sun going down behind them. Michael smiles, tilting his head up to the sky and celebrates the sun on his face, on the front of his neck, and even under his chin, tilting his head back even farther. He celebrates that the sun is still fairly warm at this stage of its sunset. He feels fortunate that this is one of the longest days of the year, and the sun is still shining down on them after this second, long, exhausting day.

He understands in an instant. He thinks about it for a moment more. He figures it out. He sees it right down beneath him. Michael even tries to do a blender laugh for T.J., but he is so tired, it comes out like a car that won't start.

Then he says to T.J. with his own smaller laugh attached to the words, "What would you say if I told you we just got X-rayed?"

T.J. cracks back at him with a silly line of her own, "I would tell you we just got our tonsils out and to give me some ice cream. We might as well imagine a good meal before we go marching into this darkness."

Michael is now swinging T.J.'s arm gleefully up and down while holding her hand without even realizing it. "No, look right behind you. Look right where we are standing. Look down on the ground where we walked past those four trees. We just walked through an X-ray machine. I see it. Look. Look at the X!"

Chapter 43

The four trees stand motionless. After T.J. slowly turns around to look at them, she stands motionless as well. T.J. says, "All I know is I'm starting to feel starvation."

Michael says, "Now I find that interesting."

T.J. replies, "You find starvation interesting?"

"No," Michael answers and then clarifies. "How the v turns into an X. I find that interesting."

Michael observes the sun cast a shadow down in the open area between the first four trees and the intimidating forest behind them. The setting sun hits the split trunk directly and creates a shadow of the "v" section down on the ground. The "v" from the tree trunk and the "v" from the shadow connect at the midpoint of both v's. The two "v's" come together, and they form an X on the ground right in front of the tree. The X right at Michael and T.J.'s feet.

"It is the sun rays that actually make the X," Michael explains as he stares at the sight to piece together how this X appears before them. He studies where the tree divides off into two separate trunks. "The sun brings a shadow of that v part down to the ground. That shadow beneath the tree creates the reverse image of the "V." see it." He points to the "∧" on the ground. The Two v's together make a clear X. Michael turns to T.J. and says in pure excitement, "Don't say we can't. Say, We Can. We Will. Just like the Buffalo Soldiers."

T.J. says, "These guys were smart! The Buffalo Soldiers were very smart, weren't they? Are you sure we are related?" Michael says, "Yes they were, and we are. We just did number four and number five from the map, just one more to go."

"Four and five, talk about getting ahead of yourself. I don't think we ever did four. I hope we don't have to go back and do it."

Michael explains further. "It isn't Cover Beehive or uncover Beehive. It is "C" Climb over beehive. It is just like the other first letters representing a full word. These guys were geniuses. We had to get to the top of the beehives to be able to notice the first four trees were out in front of the bigger forest. The X is created by the setting rays of the sun. Number five. X-Ray late day."

It comes together for Michael clearly as he points back toward the beehive mounds talking to T.J., "From up on the beehives, we probably could have even seen the X if we weren't lying down and hiding. But only by climbing over the beehive was this clearing highly visible. At ground level, the trees just blend together. T.J. is in shock but manages to say, "pretty cool!"

"Yes, we just did it. We got Number four and five from the last map at the same time. Just one more to go!"

Michael is right. You can see the X from the top of the beehives. And that is where The Big H and Miss Visor are now standing atop their beehive mound construction. The Big H has his binoculars out. Peering through them, he sees both Michael and T.J. moving toward an X in the highly visible open area. He turns to Miss Visor and says, "We are moving to our next stop. These kids are running out of numbers on the list. There has to be treasure right down there. They look pretty excited about something."

Chapter 44

The two cousins walk to the middle of the X.

"X marks the spot, right?" T.J. says as she is still in awe of their latest discovery. She turns her worries to the final number on the map's list.

6. I + Would + Not = Enter

T.J. speaks up first, "I believe what the map says this time. Unless you want to enter some hungry bear's home while they are looking for dinner, we better be careful."

Michael says, "We know that they are not exact directions. They are clues, secret ones, with hidden meanings."

He states with confidence. "I would not enter means we have to enter. We have to go into the forest. It is meant to sound scary, but I think it is telling us you have to go in. This is the map of not following the directions. If you follow what it says, you get off track."

T.J. says. "The map of misdirection. That is why I am so good at it. But I don't want to hike, I want to eat—"

T.J. can't even finish the sentence before Michael leads her by the hand and jumps high into the huge set of trees in front of them with flying on his mind. "Hey, wait, I…" she begins, but her voice disappears in the large forest as Michael lands and pulls her along. "These are the biggest trees we have seen yet. They are so big this forest has more space between each tree. This is no hike; it will be a walk in the park." He is happy.

There is no trail, but the hike is easier, and they swiftly reach a second clearing. It is perfectly round. Some trees have been removed to create this clearing. A few tree stumps remain here and there. There are smaller trees and large trees that go up overhead to create the circle. They stop to look around and take note of their surroundings. Both tiredly sit down on a tree stump toward the middle of the open area. T.J. says, "I feel like we are being watched." She is not talking about the two villains although they are not far behind.

The Big H and Miss Visor reach the X on the ground past the four guardian trees. They believe the x must mark the spot for the treasure.

Miss Visor says, "The kids ran off to escape from us when they saw us coming like they always do. We have time to dig." The Big H says, "There is one more clue, what do you think?"

Miss Visor already has a small shovel in hand and is digging away at the ground with great venom. She speaks as dirt is flying left and right. "This X must be where something is buried. You probably have to dig up a key and the clue is saying you should not enter without it! Let's start digging."

The Big H says, "You might be onto something." He

takes out the sharp walking stick from Miss Visor's pack, unfolds it, and starts to pry away at the dirt.

He stops and says, "I'm not sure. You dig. I will investigate," as he looks off in the direction of where Michael and T.J. went into the forest.

Chapter 45

M ichael and T.J. sit. They both look at the huge trees that appear to go up a mile in the sky. Michael thinks of a book he read when he was younger where he saw a picture of a car driving through a giant sequoia tree. "We have come so far," he says.

T.J. says, "We entered the forest when it told us not to. Now what happens?"

She can barely even sing to herself, so she quietly starts to hum, "Cruel Summer" while Michael continues to think. T.J. takes a break after humming the chorus a few times and again says, "I know we are being watched out in the open here."

Michael says, "We are being watched and being followed by The Big H and Miss Visor. You're right. We have to move soon," T.J. says while looking at one of the trees in front of them, "Not only is that a problem around here; even the trees are watching us."

Michael thinks. *It is more than a map. It is not a simple set of directions. It is more a set of hidden instructions.* He then says out loud, "Like we said before, an odd list. A very odd list."

T.J. quietly whispers, "Wacko, even," As the last map comes out again.

1. Ron Willis

2. Son Gilliam

3. Eat Berries

4. Cover Beehive

5. X-Ray Late Day

6. I + Would + Not = Enter

They both stare down at the map and up at the trees circling around them. Michael asks T.J., "Read each word from number six on the last map to me, one at a time. These trees are looking at us. Strange."

T.J. reads, "I would not enter."

Michael asks again, "Say it slower, much slower."

T.J. says each word with two seconds between each.

"I

would

not

Enter."

Michael repeats slowly keying into the natural land his ancestors patrolled.

"I

would

not

enter."

Michael stands up and walks forward and repeats. "I would not enter."

He looks down at the last map. I + would + not = Enter is staring back up at him from the map. T.J. stands up beside Michael and follows.

The tree they are looking at while walking is looking back at them. It is a tree with a large knot in it. The center of the knot has a dark spot with an eye shape to it. Just above the knot there is shading on the tree bark. The shading is slightly arched and is right where an eyebrow would be. It looks like an eerie eye staring directly at them.

"Homonyms, ah, homophones" Michael concludes as his mind races back to Mrs. Grand's class, and the work he did in school during a year that feels like a different universe now. "Yes, homophones," he confirms out loud.

T.J. says in a weary voice, "You want me to hum again?"

"No. Don't. Keep quiet about it, T.J. Just listen to what I am saying. Look at that big knot in the tree staring at us and say it slowly with me. "I would not enter." They both confirm the words aloud together. "I would not enter."

Michael continues to speak, "Think about it like it is written. I + would + not = Enter. Homophones. They sound the same but are spelled different and have different meanings.

"Ooooh," comes from T.J. as Michael keys her young mind into the puzzle.

"Eye + Wood + Knot = Enter. It is brilliant and tricky. The Buffalo Soldiers did it again. They aren't saying don't enter. They are saying Eye + Wood + K-n-o-t tells you exactly where to Enter." Michael is grateful.

T.J. looks like she is in a staring contest with the tree

and thinks she can win as she tilts her head sideways and gets closer and closer to the knot in the tree.

T.J. says each word separately, "Eye wood knot enter." Michael takes over the phrase, "Eye, Wood, Knot. It is all right here." He points to the tree. "There is a perfect eye right there looking at us. It is made from the knot in the wood of the tree. It is a perfect eye shape. I would not enter. It is the opposite action one more time and tells you where to enter. You said we are being watched. Yes, we are, by the knot in the wood shaped like an eye. These Buffalo soldiers were like secret agents of the woods or something. They knew everything about nature. This is it. We have done it!"

Chapter 46

Michael and T.J. are now moving up almost on top of the knot in the tree. They are slowed from walking right next to the tree by a few green bushes of wildlife surrounding the big tree at its base. The closer they get, the more amazed they are at how much the knot in the tree looks like an eye.

T.J. is the first to state what they are both thinking. "I wonder how we are going to enter a tree? Do we really have this last clue figured out?" They circle the tree. T.J. sees it first. It is almost impossible to notice unless you are as close to the ground as the tiny T.J.

On the opposite side of where the eye knot in the tree is, under one of the bushes, they see a light brown wire mesh at the base of the tree. It looks like a small fishnet and blends in perfectly with the color of the tree. It is covered with leaves and twigs and sticks that twist and turn in the wire screen and attach to it. It is easy to miss or even walk right over it unless you are right down by the ground.

T.J. says, "I just found the way in."

Michael perks up with surprise in his voice, "What? How? What do you see? How do you know it is the way in?" T.J. says as a matter of fact, "Because I'm looking at a screen door."

It is more like a window screen covering a slight opening at the bottom of the tree. Michael and T.J. don't waste any time and begin to kick away at the bottom center of the big tree where a section has been covered with a hardly visible screen. Behind the screen is a sheet of nylon fabric.

They begin jumping on the screen. Michael then uses the backpack to get more grip and pull away at the edges where the screen is somehow attached to the tree.

T.J. is so happy to have found the secret entrance and been a major part of the team that she calls on the last of her kid energy. She is now climbing up the base of the tree as far as she can and jumping down directly on the screen. "Timberrrrr," she yells each time she comes down on the screen.

Michael tells T.J. to "Look out for a second, stand back, and quiet down." He uses his pocketknife to pry at the edges of the screen. He works around half of the screen when the knife folds shut just missing his finger.

T.J. sees the near-miss of the knife snapping back in place, almost cutting Michael's finger and says, "Do you want to use my spoon?"

T.J. takes the break in Michael's action as a sign for her to continue her jumping efforts. Finally, after a few more quiet screams of "Timber," T.J.'s efforts pay off.

T.J. smashes through the screen. She takes on minor scratches as she falls halfway in a hole at the bottom of the tree. Michael continues using his backpack to pull the screen further apart to help T.J. climb back out. In a bolt, T.J. ducks down and goes further inside the tree!

"A lot of space in here," she calls up to Michael.

After all they have been through, Michael only has enough wits about him to say, "I hope Alice and Wonderland has a theme song." He then moves into older cousin mode and looks over the situation. "I can't fit all the way in; the screen is hard to pry open. T.J., be careful. These big trees can have some deep hollow places in them."

He reaches in and down as he calls T.J.'s name hoping she is alright. He feels nothing but air. Michael's arm reaches deep into the tree. His entire shoulder is inside the base of the tree. Something reaches up toward him. It touches his arm first. It is cold and has a snake-like feel. It may be dangerous. It wraps around his arm. It is tangled around his arm and is now weighing him down. Michael is about to scream.

He hears T.J.'s voice say, "You got that." And she says, "Throw down a flashlight." She is handing an item up to Michael by a ribbon that is sticking out of a canvas bag the size of AuntMom's biggest purse. "Yes, I have it," he says, "but do I want it?" He hands a flashlight down to T.J. and watches as it turns on.

T.J. says, "There are two more bags just like that one down here and some other boxes wrapped in plastic. All three heavy bags have a ribbon coming out of them. The first ribbon is now wrapped well enough around Michael's arm so that he can pull it up. It is an old well-constructed knapsack bag.

Michael says, "Climb out of there." Right after he pulls

his arm out and reaches back in to help her. It is a bit of a struggle, but T.J. makes it out with Michael's help. She doesn't look much dirtier than when she went in. T.J. exits the base of the tree with one more bag besides the one she handed up to Michael.

They have a prize in hand. They both look incredibly worn and tired. But they feel like a million dollars. Who knows, they may have a million dollars of treasure in their hands. Michael lightly tosses the bag a few inches up in the air and lets it fall back down victoriously in his hands. They are both celebrating the weight inside each bag. They definitely have something that feels like treasure, a lot of treasure. Michael says, "I don't even remember where this journey began, but it looks like we have made it to the end together."

Chapter 47

It gets late in the summer evening. The bottom edge of the sun starts to trend below the horizon. Miss Visor begins to tire and become more aggravated. She doesn't have the best digging tools but creates a bunch of random holes as the "X" on the ground moves and stretches out in shadow form and grows longer as the sun sets.

Miss Visor screams to The Big H who has returned from his investigation, "Should we try to come back with a metal detector?"

The Big H says, "No, we are close. I went around the perimeter of the trees and didn't see anything or hear anything. They have hit every map marker on the list. It isn't about knowing what's on the map. We need the map–it is giving them something with these clues that we aren't getting. Or that crazy uncle of theirs has given them some secret hints. We need to get the other clues off the map or get the kids or get both."

Miss Visor says, "Okay, let's move out into the forest. Split up. Don't be afraid to get up in the trees and put those binoculars to work before we lose the last of our daylight. We always do better looking for those little runts from higher ground. They are almost impossible to track at ground level in a bunch of trees."

The Big H peers into the forest, scanning for Michael and T.J. He is unable to see anything or hear anything. He heads off in one direction, and Miss Visor heads off in the other.

Michael and T.J. are both holding onto the old knapsack and massaging their fingers around the bag to feel, in case it is something dangerous. They believe it is something glorious. They can't tell for sure, but Michael says, "We actually have the treasure of the last map in our hands. We open our bags and lay out the belongings together on three. That means one, two, three, then open." T.J. says, "Okay That is how you communicate a countdown." She takes a breath and blows some cool air up toward her forehead and adds, "I'm ready." Michael takes a few deep short breaths of his own and begins the count, "One, two, three."

They untie their bags, and Michael reaches in and pulls out a folder sized item wrapped in thick plastic. It feels like a picture frame. T.J. begins to dump her entire bag out at their feet. After Michael takes out the item wrapped in plastic, he more carefully empties out his bag by shaking everything out as well. He turns the bag over and shakes it carefully for some time. A collection of items comes tumbling out of the bags. Boxes come out first. They look like presentation boxes and a few large jewelry boxes. A few papers fall out as well. More items fall down out of the bag, wrapped in cloth and heavy paper and in plastic coverings. Then one box hits the ground and springs open. A second box does the same and a ringing sound fills the air as two pieces of metal hit each other.

Michael and T.J. look down at a gold and silver coin right next to each other. They both dive down to the ground and unbox and uncover each piece without stopping for a nanosecond. They finally finish this ultimate Christmas morning unboxing. They both lean back against the tree and see gold coins, then silver coins, then beautiful crosses and smaller coins. It is a true treasure. Michael says it aloud so the universe understands, "The Last Map is real!"

Chapter 48

T.J. moves her head in agreement. No song, no chorus, no verse, she only says, "The last map is going to get AuntMom a new house." She hesitates and then continues, "Too bad we will probably have to live in the basement on permanent time-out in that house." They now examine the joyful collection in front of them and think of the other bag and boxes still in the tree. She is looking at Michael now. "Why are all of the bigger coins attached to ribbons?" Michael already has a couple of items in his hands that he is examining. "They aren't coins. They are medals, and awards and wait; a few do look like they are coins. An old silver dollar, and a few that look like pennies. This one says, 'half-cent' on it.'"

T.J. says, "'Half-cent'. Wow! We better hide that one from AuntMom. My allowance is already too low. I'm sure she would pay me in half-cents if she could. I mean of all the luck to have—we uncover a treasure worth a half-cent!"

Michael says, "There is another penny with a Native American face on it. These are maybe a hundred years old or more. I know they are worth a lot, T.J. These aren't your ordinary fountain pennies."

Michael then brings his attention back to the folder. He alerts T.J. to his find, "This is sealed in thick plastic." He stands up tall to open it. Again, he has to use his pocket knife. This time he is ultra-careful and cuts around the edges of the thick plastic and some tape. T.J. is arranging the medals magnificently. Some are wrapped in cloth, some in smaller bags, some in boxes, and some in plastic with paper inside. The ribbon and all of the medals are in surprisingly great shape and great color. T.J. is trying to set up a distinct order on the ground before she places them. She has put two medals around her neck and places a medal around Michael's neck. They both look very honorary.

T.J. asks, "Does it say how many millions these coins are worth?"

Michael peels away the thick plastic and gets down to a neatly presented letter. T.J. stands up next to Michael just as he begins to read:

We have seen the traumas of war to both sides and all suffer. We have experienced the broken promises of politicians. When we returned to our cities and communities we were not acknowledged and awarded as others were.

We were fine with that in a way because we fought for our children. We knew our children would have it better.

Our hopes ended when our sons, daughters, grandsons, and granddaughters served in not one but two World wars. They returned from war and were denied their promised pathway to education, home ownership, and guaranteed care.

We have seen returning warriors from all creeds and all commands treated worse as the days and years pass.

Who protects the protectors?

We traveled the world because of this great military. The land we were charged to protect remains, to us, the most beautiful. We returned here to these lands with our medals, accommodations, memories, and artifacts of service.

They are buried here on these grounds, in the last place we were most respected and the place that respected us the most.

We are proud and honored to have served, but the end results and treatment of soldiers and the rights they fought for continues to be corrupted.

We hope that by the time future generations resolve the last map and our medals are unearthed, freedom and respect for returning personnel and the rights they die for will be established and retained.

We leave our medals here, for now.

To all:
    We Can, We Will

Sincerely,

The Last Act of the Buffalo Soldiers
    – Caretakers of the State Parks we have manned and created for all – for as long as the shores shall stand.

"O-80 is going to want to read this." The excitement in Michael's voice is undeniable, but he can't bring himself to say anything else. The last map has been solved, but

Michael quietly feels like he has solved something more for his family. He stares downward to reread the letter to examine every word.

T.J. says, "Well, cousin, we might just get out of here to show him. Over there, way over there, look, there are lights!"

Chapter 49

As the sun goes halfway down, one or two small lights start to appear in the distance through another set of trees down in a low dark valley.

"It is light for sure, but it is far away," Michael says as he looks out in the distance.

The lights seem to be swaying back and forth "It may be from a small campsite. Maybe some lanterns on a wire hung up by a camp. Maybe it is even a store or two down there. Or a home or two or even a search party."

T.J. says, "Maybe they have a restaurant or more than one restaurant down there. We need to eat, and we need to eat more than once."

The lights are moving down below in the next valley. However, they have marched through much worse over the last two days. They collect the set of medals and items and put them back in the bags. They cover the tree opening well. It almost looks undisturbed, as they begin to walk forward. They each have a bag in hand. They only go a few paces beyond the inner circle of trees when they see a major problem. There is a huge gap between two cliffs to get from where they are to the other side and begin the long walk down toward the lights.

They walk forward and reach the edge of a gorge that goes on for miles. They look and see how far it is to cross. There is a sizable trench between them and their path to reach the lights. They don't see a bridge or rope, and T.J. adds with frustration in her voice,

"I would even take a vine. It would be nice to swing across." They walk along the side of the gorge hoping for a fallen tree to help them across. They go up and down the ridge and see the two lights across and over the crest of a small hill on the other side. They look at the lights down below from every angle as they walk. The lights still sway back and forth.

"I don't know how far away the lights are on the other side of the hill, and why they are rolling back and forth. But they are the most light we have seen in two days, and it has to be someone or some place." Michael is building the team's confidence.

"We must find a way to get across."

T.J. says, "Can we signal down with the flashlight?"

Michael calculates, "Our flashlight was barely strong enough to see inside the tree. There is no way it is going to shine bright enough to be seen all the way over there, but you can try it. When in doubt, I look at the map, right?"

Michael pulls out the last map that he has placed in the same folder as the letter from the Buffalo Soldiers. He pulls it out of the bag and pulls out a big medal again. He is still amazed looking at their achievement. The more they are in hand, the more the reality of their accomplishment comes into light. T.J. picks one out of the bag as well. "Really cool, cousin. Really cool!" They feel triumphant. They will make it. "These medals show we completed the last map. We can do anything together. We have to find a way over the large cliff."

Both raise the medals like a toast on New Year's Eve and 'clink' them together as Michael is finding the energy to give one last full motivational speech. They hold them up high like they are on an Olympic platform earning their first gold.

The sunset is just beyond halfway down. The pair create a beautiful silhouette with the remaining sunlight. They are feeling victorious, holding up the medals. T.J. begins a tired dance step or two. The long lines of light reach across the sky, shine on the medals being held up high and gleam like solid gold.

The late-day sunlight reflects directly off the medals. The flashes of light give away their exact location to The Big H. He is a few feet up in a tree searching for them. He is positioned to their far left with Miss Visor on their far, far right looking in an even more intense manner. The Big H looks up by the gorge and confirms what he sees through his quickly rising binoculars.

"They got OUR gold in THEIR hands! The Big H calls in a low rumbling voice to Miss Visor even though she is too far away to hear him. He raises his voice. "We are not leaving this mess without getting PAID, now!"

The Big H abruptly pulls out his gun. He isn't inter- ested in chasing anymore, but he is not prepared to fire a shot directly at two children. He makes his anger clear with a gunshot high into the trees from his revolver. The shot wasn't menacing. It wasn't cool. It wasn't anything you would associate with courage. It was random and soulless. It was the sound of a deadly, emotionless voice. Michael and T.J. are shot above once, and then shot nearer as the second shot is aimed lower and flies through the trees. It is cold, and it is chilling. It causes Miss Visor to look up from across the trees and grin. She starts running hard in the direction The Big H is shooting.

When the first gunshot is heard, T.J.'s little face freezes. Michael shakes, and they both approach the gorge. Michael immediately considers flying across but doesn't want to leave T.J.

They consider climbing down, "But down to where?" T.J. shakes uncontrollably as she asks Michael.

The gorge looks bottomless. They see a small ledge they may be able to jump onto, but one misstep and they are gone for sure. It is getting dark, and the ledge can only barely be seen. They try to double back when the second shot comes.

Gunshots are scary, even if you are expecting one. The loud "POW" and crack sound like a twelve-foot whip. The sound that comes after lingers in the air. This is absolutely frightening. In the forest, the sound echoes, and Michael and T.J. hear a few animals scurry away by instinct. They do the same and begin to duck behind rocks and through trees to escape the determined sound of a bullet looking to land.

There weren't many places for Michael and T.J. to run and hide with the gorge right behind them and the trees in this section of the forest not close together. They both know the procedure to escape The Big H and Miss Visor. They keep in the tree line and behind a couple of the bigger trees and rocks as best they can.

The Big H says as he fires a third general shot up above them. "It ain't personal, kid. It's collecting a find." The third shot calls out with a terrible, terrible sound.

Chapter 50

To hear the terrible, terrible sound is one thing. To look down and see your cousin, the boy who thinks he can fly, Michael Jefferson put on the ground with a true real-life wound is another thing.

The red blood is immediate. It is thick and sticky like glue. Michael is down low to hide from the villains. He is forced to take a seat back against one of the bigger trees. He sits still in the forest to try to slow the madness. He is not feeling anything but tingling in his low back and legs. His legs feel powerless. The blood clings to T.J.'s fingers as soon she reaches down and examines what is happening. T.J. can't shake the red off as she frantically moves her fingers back and forth trying to make the blood go away. It is stuck there on her fingers and on Michael's clothes, on Michael's leg reminding T.J. that this is real. It is not like television where they get shot then get up and go home. Not like the movies where it is cool to get shot because it just makes you mad enough to get really tough. Not like video games where you get shot and then go back and start over at the beginning of the level.

Michael Jefferson is slouching down to his side against the big tree. His eyes look like glass. They appear as if they are going to crack like a windshield that has just been struck by a small but powerful rock. Michael looks up at T.J. and looks at her face and says, "I'm sorry about what happened to your Mom and Dad, but I'm your best friend. I'll be with you. Michael just has the strength to finally say, "Just run, run as fast as you can; climb down the gorge.

"No, it's too far down," T.J. says.

As he glances toward the gorge, "Go, go, you can make it." Michael encourages T.J. to "Run!– Tell AuntMom, tell my mom I love her, and she makes great cookies. But you go from here without me. I can lie here and cover myself. I can even maybe crawl and sneak back and hide in the Buffalo Soldiers' tree. You get away like we always do. You bring back help for me. It is our best chance. You can't carry me. Just RUN!" Michael strains his voice through the pain in his side.

T.J. begins to try and drag Michael to safety as she sees The Big H stomping down from the ridge they were just on and getting in closer range. Miss Visor is coming up from the other direction as Michael yells out in pain and grabs at his messy side as it turns deep red. T.J. says desperately, eyes tearing up now. "I can't make it without you–I'll, I'll never make it–I ca-can't make it."

Michael jumps in and continues, "We have the medals. We completed the last map of the Buffalo Soldiers. O-80 will be back!"

Before Michael Jefferson closes his eyes, seemingly to

never be heard from again, he touches his friend T.J.'s hand and says, "I give you my power to fly. I would have flown out of here myself earlier, but I didn't want to leave you behind. When you fly, I'll fly, and we'll both be very happy." Michael Jefferson slowly moves both arms up in front of his head as if he is taking flight and says, "I give you my power to fly."

T.J. watches her best friend's eyes close. She wants to sing a sad song. She moves her mouth, but this one time, her voice delivers no words.

Frightened by the stillness of her cousin, her friend, her defender, T.J. tries to move closer but can't. She looks at the best part of her remaining family lying silent and creeps back slowly away from Michael as if walking backward would make the world travel in reverse and everything would be okay.

She steps back and back and back and would have walked backward for the rest of her life to back out of the dreadful reality she now faces. She keeps going until she backs into a big tree and is stopped by the rough cadence of the bark on her small, tired back. And then CRACK! The sudden alarm of a fourth shot comes, and the bark far above her head crumbles down on top of her head, onto her hat and her hair. The Big H yells, "Stop, kid, Stop! Drop everything."

T.J. does not stop. She tears off her hat. She doesn't feel like giving The Big H a maroon target so close to her head. She hangs her hat on a branch a few yards away, hoping to mislead The Big H, and ducks down low behind a tree. She thinks to herself, *that is something smart Michael would do* as she looks at him, with his eyes mostly closed, resting against the tree. She also thinks this will help mark where Michael is hiding so she can come back for him. She takes one direct step to race through the forest the same way they were heading, but she sees Miss Visor coming toward her so fast and hardcore that she hears her breathing and huffing and puffing like an asthmatic wolf.

T.J. is scared. She runs off in the other direction, running along the ridge of the gorge as fast as she can, with the howling Miss Visor behind her.

Miss Visor snarls like a wolverine. Both she and The Big H come together and are closing in on T.J. from both sides. The Big H says, "I don't want to end these kids, but I won't end without the treasure." He slowly lowers his gun, stepping cautiously near the gorge but moving on with good speed.

T.J. has no choice. She will jump down, likely to never be heard from again. She drops the bag of medals, but she still has two medals around her neck and grabs three more with ribbons to wrap around her arms. She will know that she has the treasure with her on the way down. And that they completed the last map when she hits the bottom. Maybe she will get to go see her mom.

She would like to put a medal around her mom's neck, too. She looks back before she makes the jump into the deep gorge. If she lands perfectly, maybe she can climb down and hide, but then what? She has no food and no water. She is at the end of nowhere. T.J. is about to plunge over the side never to be heard from again.

She looks back and can't find Michael within the trees, but she knows he is watching her like he always does. She finds tears in her eyes and the blurry lights swaying in the distance. The sun is all but gone now with just a bit of light struggling to reach the top of the ridge. T.J. looks down into the gorge, and it is almost total darkness. She only has room for one more step. She has no idea where she is going to land, but she jumps…

Maybe it is the wind—an uptick from the gusts on the canyon floor. Possibly through the caves. A strong rush of air caught between baggy clothes. Or a little boy who gave away his power to fly.

T.J. flies up in the air. Up almost unbelievably high into the skyline of the two swaying lights in the distance. So high The Big H stops in his tracks and Miss Visor falls to her knees in disbelief, hyperventilating from shock and running so hard to catch up to the gleaming medals. T.J. tumbles in the air, medals still swinging in hand. She rolls over mid-flight. She laughs when she is upright, thinking of how happy Michael always looks when he launches himself up into the air. She tumbles backward in mid-air, gets caught in her own clothing trying to stick her arm out, thinking she can control her majestic flight. She continues for one last moment, and then launches downward with a stumbling hop when she lands on the other side of the cliff's edge. She rolls down a few feet before she is able to look back and see how far she flew and gets up and runs. She runs fast, singing more off note than ever. She tells herself, two days in a forest will do that to your voice. She is singing so loud she knows her Mom, Dad, Aunt, and Cousin have to hear every word. She keeps running and singing until she reaches the two lights of a small search party drone drifting back and forth, shining down into her face.

Michael's eyes close down to small slits. He strains to

keep them that way to see the fate of his cousin. His eyes follow her, and he looks up and into the air when she flies. His eyes blow wide open, as wide as they possibly can. Seeing T.J. stick her arm out in flight, he smiles, not in disbelief, but in full belief. He throws his free hand out... the hand not holding his damaged side. It moves strongly out in front of him like he is riding the sky.

Ladies and gentlemen, friends, Michael Jefferson is flying.

Fortunately, singing T.J. gets away safely.

-*Will she be in trouble forever?*

Michael Jefferson is flying.

-*Do his feet ever touch the ground again?*

The Big H is still The Big H.

-*But The Big H doesn't stand for what The Big H stood for before.*

Miss Visor is still mean.

-*Absolutely no surprise there.*

AuntMom is still nice.

- *(but everybody is in trouble with her—probably forever, including 0-80).*

0-80 knows the truth!

-*Find the answers to these questions, clues, and more when the Last Map concludes…*

Enjoy this book?

You can make a big difference.

Reviews are the most powerful method to share
the fun I have writing these stories.

If you had fun with The Last Map, I would be
grateful if you could leave a review.

.

Also by John Newsom

The Xtrodinaries Book 1
Theo Lord of the Fries

The Xtrodinaries Book 2
Rina Much Ado About Netting

Join the reading group at: JohnNewsom.com